Constance Santego

Constance Santego
Beneath the Vineyards

Dr. Constance Santego weaves stories of love, history, and personal transformation set against the breathtaking landscapes of British Columbia. Living in the heart of Canada's Okanagan Valley, she draws inspiration from the beauty around her to create compelling narratives that explore the intricacies of the human spirit. Constance shares a fulfilling life with her husband, and her work reflects her passion for storytelling, healing, and the enduring power of connection.

www.constancesantego.ca

Published by
Editor & Interior Layout: Dr. Constance Santego
Book Layout: ©2017 BookDesignTemplates.com
Soft Cover ISBN: 978-1-990062-51-3
eBook ISBN: 978-1-990062-52-0

Created and published in Canada. Printed and bound in the United States of America
Ordering Information: csantego@gmail.com

ALSO BY DR. CONSTANCE SANTEGO

NOVELS
Illegitamate Grace

The Nine Spiritual Gifts Series:
Journey of a Soul – (Vol 1 Michael)
Language of a Soul – (Vol 2 Gabriel)
Prophecy of a Soul – (Vol 3 Bath Kol)
Healing of a Soul – (Vol 4 Raphael)
Miracles of a Soul – (Vol 5 Hamied)
Knowledge of a Soul – (Vol 6 Raziel)
Wisdom of a Soul – (Vol 7 Uriel)
Faith of a Soul – (Vol 8 Uriel)

NONFICTION
The Intuitive Life, The Gift Of Prophecy, Third Edition
Fairy Tales, Dreams And Reality… Where Are You On Your Path? Second Edition
Your Persona… The Mask You Wear
Angelic Lifestyle, a Vibrant Lifestyle
Angelic Lifestyle 42-Day Energy Cleanse
Archangel Michael's Soul Retrieval Guide
Tesla And The Future Of Energy Medicine
Beyond Tesla: *Advancing The Science Of Energy Healing*
Tesla's Code: *Mastering Energy, Frequency, And Creative Power*
Scaling Beyond 6 Figures: *Strategies for Health & Wellness Professionals*
Beyond the Mind: *Harnessing the Power of Astral Projection*

for Creative Awakening
Bend, Don't Break: *Finding Your Way Back to Abundance*
Ring Therapy: *A Guide to Healing and Balance*
Ring Therapy Pocket Guide
Floraopathy™: *The Art and Science of Vibrational Healing with Essential Oils*

SECRETS OF A HEALER, SERIES:
Magic Of Aromatherapy (Vol I)
Magic Of Reflexology (Vol II)
Magic Of The Gifts (Vol III)
Magic Of Muscle Testing (Vol IV)
Magic Of Iridology (Vol V)
Magic Of Massage (Vol VI)
Magic Of Hypnotherapy (Vol VII)
Magic Of Reiki (Vol VIII)
Magic Of Advanced Aromatherapy (Vol IX)
Magic Of Esthetics (Vol X)
The Reiki Master's Manual (Vol XI)

ADULT COLORING JOURNALS
SERIES-ZEN COLORING:
Quantum Energy and Mindful Living Journal (Vol 1)
Reiki Energy Journal (Vol 2)
Nine Spiritual Gifts Journal (Vol 3)
I Forgive Journal (Vol 4)

SERIES – COLORING PROSPERITY:
Genie-Inspired Mandalas and Wealth Journal (Vol 1)
Entrepreneurial Mindset Reboot (Vol 2)

SERIES – HARMONIC MIND CODE:
Harmonic Mind Code Coloring Journal (Vol 1)

FOR CHILDREN
I am Big Tonight. I Don't Need the Light

Dedicated

To my Okanagan ancestors, whose strength, dreams, and stories paved the way for mine. This book is a tribute to the legacy of love, resilience, and the timeless bonds that connect us all.

Beneath the Vineyards

Claire Bennett: A Journey of Love and Renewal

In the picturesque Okanagan Valley, Claire Bennett finds herself at a crossroads. A talented travel writer burdened by creative burnout and a longing to rediscover her purpose, she embarks on a journey to Kelowna, British Columbia, Canada—a land of sun-drenched vineyards, sparkling lake waters, and the promise of a fresh start.

Claire's story unfolds amid the golden hues of a grape harvest, where she meets Ethan, a winemaker dedicated to preserving his family's legacy. Their connection challenges her independence and opens her heart to new possibilities. As she immerses herself in the rhythms of vineyard life, Claire begins to see the parallels between nurturing the land and healing her own soul.

This is a tale of transformation, where love and the beauty of nature intertwine to remind us that growth often comes from life's most unexpected places. Against the vibrant backdrop of Kelowna's wine country, Claire's journey reflects the themes of resilience, connection, and the courage to embrace the unknown.

The roots of our past anchor us,

but it is in nurturing them that we find
the strength to grow, heal, and create
our own path.

Dr. Constance Santego

Fact and Disclaimer:

This novel draws inspiration from real places, traditions, and cultural elements, woven together to craft a story of love, healing, and personal growth. While the Okanagan Valley and its breathtaking vineyards serve as the vibrant setting, all characters and specific events are entirely fictional and a product of the author's imagination.

The story is designed to offer readers a fresh perspective, immersing them in the beauty of Kelowna's wine country and reflecting on the complexities of human connection, resilience, and the pursuit of purpose.

Any resemblance to actual persons, living or dead, or actual events is purely coincidental.

Prologue

The sun dipped low over the rolling hills of Kelowna, casting golden light across the sprawling vineyards. Here, amidst the rows of ripening grapes and the gentle hum of the Okanagan breeze, life seemed to slow, as though the land itself whispered stories of resilience and renewal.

I arrived here seeking neither fame nor fortune but escape. My world, once brimming with purpose, had grown cold, as though every word I wrote weighed heavier than the last. Vancouver, with its relentless pace and unyielding expectations, had drained me of the very thing that defined me, my voice.

In this valley of sunlit vines and ancient soil, I hoped to find something—a spark, a reason, perhaps even redemption. What I did not expect was him.

Ethan. A man as rooted in this land as the vines he tended, burdened by his own battles yet steadfast in his resolve. He was not the kind to offer easy answers or gentle reassurances, but through his quiet strength, I began to see the possibility of something more.

This is not a story of dramatic transformations or sweeping declarations. It is a story of quiet moments—of hands stained with grape juice, of late-night conversations beneath a canopy of stars, and of the courage it takes to let go of the past and embrace the uncertain.

Before you judge the choices that brought us here, know this: sometimes, it is in the stillness of a vineyard and the depths of a heart that we find the strength to start anew.

Sometimes, the greatest stories are not the ones we write but the ones we live.

Chapter 1

The tires crunched against the gravel driveway as Claire Bennett eased her rental car to a stop, the engine's hum fading into the vast silence of the vineyard. She gripped the steering wheel, her knuckles pale against the leather, and inhaled deeply, the tang of earth and sun-warmed grapes mingling with the lingering scent of pine drifting from the surrounding hills.

The scene before her was almost too perfect, like something plucked from a travel brochure, rows of vines stretched endlessly under a golden autumn sky, their leaves tinged with amber and crimson. Beyond the vineyard, the waters of Okanagan Lake shimmered, the afternoon sun scattering diamonds across its surface.

It should have felt like a respite, this idyllic corner of the world. Instead, Claire's chest tightened, the weight of a looming deadline pressing down on her. She was here to salvage her career, not to lose herself in scenery. Her editor's words echoed in her mind: "Bring me a story that makes people feel like they've tasted the wine, smelled the air. Make it personal, Claire. Something that matters."

Personal? Claire's laugh was dry, humorless. The only thing personal about this assignment was the desperation clinging to it. Three months ago, her publisher had rejected her latest manuscript—a blow that sent her reeling, questioning if she even deserved to call herself a writer anymore. The Kelowna assignment had been an act of mercy, a lifeline to pull her back from obscurity.

With a sigh, she stepped out of the car, her boots sinking slightly into the gravel. The air was sharp and clean, carrying the faint sweetness of ripening grapes. She slung her bag over her shoulder and glanced at the modest sign near the entrance: **Evergreen Estates Winery. Family-Owned Since 1946.**

As she approached the tasting room, a large dog—a shaggy mix of something friendly and intimidating—trotted out to greet her. It barked once, then plopped onto the ground, tail wagging.

"Nice to meet you too," Claire muttered, offering a hesitant smile as she sidestepped the enthusiastic greeter.

The wooden door creaked as she pushed it open, and the cool, earthy scent of oak barrels and fermenting wine greeted her. The interior was cozy but unpretentious, with polished wooden floors and large windows that framed the vineyard like living art.

"Can I help you?"

The voice, deep and steady, came from the far end of the room. Claire turned, her practiced greeting momentarily catching in her throat.

The man leaning against the counter was tall and broad-shouldered, his flannel shirt rolled to the elbows, revealing forearms dusted with the remnants of the day's labor. His dark hair was slightly disheveled, and a faint scruff shadowed his jawline. But it was his eyes—gray and piercing, like a storm rolling over the lake—that held her attention.

"I'm Claire Bennett," she said, forcing her voice to steady as she extended a hand. "I'm here to write about the vineyards in the region. I called earlier this week?"

Recognition flickered in his expression, followed by something harder to place—wariness, perhaps?

"Ethan," he said, shaking her hand briefly before pulling back. "Ethan Montgomery. This is my family's vineyard."

Claire glanced around the room, taking in the photographs on the wall: harvests from decades past, a black-and-white shot of a couple standing proudly in front of the very building she stood in now.

"It's beautiful," she said, meaning it.

Ethan's lips twitched, almost forming a smile before settling into a neutral line. "It's a lot of work."

There was something guarded about him, a quiet intensity that made Claire feel like she was under scrutiny. She wasn't sure if it was her city clothes, her notepad tucked conspicuously under her arm, or just the fact that she was an outsider.

"I was hoping to get a tour," she said, trying to inject warmth into her tone.

Ethan hesitated, his sharp gaze taking her in. She was about 5'6", wearing a floral dress that swayed just above her knees with the slight breeze. It wasn't tight-fitting, but it hinted at a frame that wasn't fat, skinny, or particularly fit—just comfortably her. Her dark brown hair, falling just past her shoulders, framed a face that wasn't strikingly pretty nor forgettable—more cute, with a kind of approachable charm. Hazel eyes met his with unwavering determination, the kind that made him think she'd gotten her way more than once just by holding her ground.

A worn briefcase hung at her side, adding a touch of professionalism that felt slightly at odds with the dress. Yet, the combination suited her, as if she'd carefully chosen it to blend into the relaxed charm of the valley while still commanding respect. Ethan crossed his arms, leaning back slightly. "A tour?"

"Yes," Claire said, meeting his gaze directly. "I'm writing an article for Escapes magazine. The Okanagan's wineries are the focus, and I thought Evergreen Estates would make an excellent centerpiece."

He studied her for a long moment, his expression unreadable. Finally, he pushed off the counter.

"Fine," he said, gesturing toward the door. "But keep up. I don't have time for people slowing me down."

Claire blinked, momentarily stunned by his abruptness. Then her pride kicked in, and she followed him outside, the crisp air biting at her cheeks.

"Charming," she muttered under her breath, earning a sharp glance from Ethan as he walked ahead, his strides long and purposeful.

She hurried after him, determined not to let his brusque demeanor get under her skin. This wasn't about making friends. It was about the story.

As they walked through the rows of sunlit vines, Ethan glanced sideways at Claire, his expression unreadable. The silence between them was punctuated by the occasional rustle of leaves and the hum of bees busy with the late-season blooms.

"So, Bennett," he said finally, the hint of a smile tugging at the corner of his mouth. "Any chance you're related to *those* Bennetts?"

Claire blinked, caught off guard. "Those Bennetts?"

He stopped walking and turned to face her fully, one brow arching in mild amusement. "You know, the William R. Bennett Bridge? Former Premier Bill Bennett? Kind of a big name around here."

Claire laughed softly, shaking her head. "No relation, as far as I know. Though I'd love to claim credit for a bridge that iconic."

Ethan's smile widened, though it was brief, like the flash of sunlight between clouds. "Figures. You don't strike me as someone tied to politics or pontoon bridges."

"Not exactly," she said, gesturing toward her notepad tucked under her arm. "More words than infrastructure. Though I have to admit, I'm impressed you brought it up. History buff?"

"Hardly," he replied, starting to walk again. "But when you grow up here, you can't escape the stories. The Bennetts are a part of Kelowna's identity, like the lake or the vineyards." He glanced at her again, this time with a touch of curiosity. "Thought maybe you were a part of that legacy."

Claire smiled, a little wistfully. "No bridges or big names in my family, just a lot of restless wanderers. Guess that's why I'm here."

Ethan nodded thoughtfully but didn't press further. The moment lingered, quiet but significant, as they both turned their attention back to the vineyard, the air between them filled with something unspoken yet undeniably shared.

Chapter 2

Claire stared at the blank page of her notepad, her pen hovering uselessly above the paper. She had always loved beginnings—the crisp possibilities of a fresh start, the first threads of a story pulling her into its world. But here, surrounded by the intoxicating scents of soil and grapes, the words refused to come.

The tasting room had grown quieter as the late afternoon sun dipped lower in the sky. Ethan had retreated to the vineyard after the briefest of tours, his departure as abrupt as his introduction. He was polite enough, she supposed, but his demeanor had all the warmth of a steel door.

With a sigh, Claire tucked her notepad into her bag and stepped outside. The golden light bathed the rows of vines, casting long shadows across the ground. She hadn't lied earlier—the place was beautiful. But beauty alone wouldn't write her article.

She wandered aimlessly, the crunch of gravel underfoot her only companion. Ahead, the vines gave way to an open clearing where a small group of workers gathered, their laughter and chatter drifting toward her on the breeze. Buckets of freshly picked grapes lined the ground, their deep purple hue almost glowing in the fading light.

"Enjoying yourself?"

The voice startled her, low and familiar. Claire turned to find Ethan leaning against a nearby post, his arms crossed and an almost-smile playing on his lips.

"I'm trying," she replied, recovering quickly. "This place is stunning, but it doesn't exactly scream 'open book.'"

Ethan raised a brow. "What's that supposed to mean?"

Claire hesitated, then decided there was little to lose by being honest. "You're not exactly chatty. Makes it hard to get the human side of the story."

He considered her words for a moment before pushing off the post and stepping closer. "The story isn't about me."

"No," she agreed, meeting his gaze. "But the story is about this place, and you're as much a part of it as the vines and the soil."

Ethan's jaw tightened, and for a moment, she thought she'd overstepped. Then he surprised her.

"Come with me," he said, gesturing toward the clearing.

Claire followed, her curiosity outweighing her reluctance. The workers nodded to Ethan as they passed, their easy familiarity hinting at years of trust and shared labor.

At the edge of the clearing, Ethan stopped and picked up a grape cluster from one of the buckets. He held it out to her.

"Taste it."

Claire hesitated, then plucked a grape and popped it into her mouth. The flavor burst across her tongue—sweet and rich with a slight tang, like the essence of sunshine captured in fruit.

"It's incredible," she said, her voice softer than she intended.

Ethan nodded, his expression unreadable. "That's what we work for. Every grape, every season, comes down to moments like this."

Claire looked at him, suddenly seeing the weight of his words. There was more to Ethan than his brusque exterior. She could see it now—in the way his hand lingered on the grapevine, the way his voice softened when he talked about the land.

"Why do you do it?" she asked quietly.

His gaze met hers, steady and unflinching. "Because it matters. This place, this work—it's not just about making wine. It's about carrying something forward. My family started this vineyard with nothing but grit and a belief that they could create something lasting. I'm not about to let that go."

Claire felt a twinge of envy at his conviction. She had spent so much time chasing stories, searching for meaning, that she hadn't realized how rootless she'd become.

"And you?" he asked, breaking the silence. "Why do you do what you do?"

She hesitated. The easy answer—because I love writing—felt hollow. The truth was messier, tangled in doubt and fear.

"I guess I'm still figuring that out," she admitted.

Ethan studied her for a moment, then nodded, as though he understood more than she'd said. "Well, if you're going to write about this place, you should see all of it. Harvest starts at dawn tomorrow. Be here if you want to learn what this place is really about."

Claire blinked, caught off guard by the unexpected invitation. "Dawn? That's—"

"Early," Ethan finished, a hint of a smile returning. "But it's worth it. Your call."

He turned and walked back toward the workers, leaving Claire standing in the clearing with the taste of sweet grapes still on her tongue and the faintest glimmer of hope taking root in her chest.

Chapter 3

The first rays of sunlight crept over the hills, painting the Okanagan Valley in soft golds and pinks. Claire stood amidst the rows of vines, her boots sinking slightly into the dew-dampened soil. The air was crisp, carrying a faint chill that made her draw her jacket tighter, but it was clean and alive, laced with the scent of earth, grass, and the faint sweetness of grapes ripening on the vine.

Before her, Okanagan Lake stretched out like polished glass, its surface barely disturbed except for the occasional ripple from a passing breeze. The water shimmered under the soft morning light, reflecting the golden and rose hues of the sky in a breathtaking display of nature's artistry. In the stillness, the faint hum of a fishing boat drifted across the lake, a gentle reminder that life stirred beyond the serenity.

It was stunning, a beauty so profound it seemed to press against her chest. Claire felt a pang of something she couldn't quite name—maybe longing, maybe peace, maybe both. She had spent so many years moving from one place to another, always chasing the next story, the next deadline. But here, in this quiet moment, it felt as though time had paused just for her.

She let her eyes drift across the landscape, taking in the patchwork of vineyards and orchards stretching up the slopes, the vibrant greens giving way to the deeper blues and purples of the lake and the pale blues of the sky. She'd never seen a place so effortlessly beautiful, so utterly itself.

"Not a bad way to start the day."

Ethan's voice startled her, breaking the stillness. She turned to find him a few rows away, fixing a post. His flannel shirt was unbuttoned at the collar, the sleeves rolled up to his elbows, and his hair was tousled as though he'd simply rolled out of bed and walked straight into the vineyard.

"I can see why you like it here," Claire said, gesturing toward the view.

Ethan's gaze shifted to the lake, his expression softening. "It's easy to take it for granted when you see it every day. But yeah, it's something."

Claire smiled, though she wasn't sure if it was at his words or the rare vulnerability she caught in his tone.

"Ready for harvest?" he asked, finishing off the post and walking toward her.

"As ready as I'll ever be," she replied, glancing down at her boots and wondering if they'd survive a full day of fieldwork.

Ethan smirked, catching her hesitation. "Don't worry, city girl. You'll survive."

"Thanks for the vote of confidence," Claire shot back, her tone light but her cheeks warming.

He led her deeper into the vineyard, the rows of vines seeming endless in the morning light. Workers were already busy, their movements brisk but unhurried as they filled baskets with ripe grapes. The sound of laughter and the occasional shout, spoken in a mix of English and Spanish, filled the air. These lively voices blended harmoniously with the distant call of a Steller's Jay and the gentle rustling of leaves in the breeze.

"You'll start here," Ethan said, handing her a pair of clippers. "Watch your fingers. And if you get stuck, just ask."

Claire raised an eyebrow. "You're actually trusting me with this?"

Ethan chuckled. "We'll see if that trust is misplaced."

For the next hour, Claire worked alongside the others, her movements awkward at first but growing steadier with each bunch of grapes she clipped. The work was harder than it looked—bending, reaching, careful not to crush the fruit—but there was something meditative about it. The rhythm, the quiet focus, the sense of contributing to something greater than herself.

When she paused to straighten, her back protesting slightly, she found Ethan watching her from a few rows over. He didn't say anything, just gave a small nod, as if to acknowledge that she was holding her own.

Claire turned back to the vines, a small smile tugging at her lips. She wasn't sure what had brought her to this place—to this man, to this land—but for the first time in a long time, she felt like she was exactly where she needed to be.

Chapter 4

The sun climbed higher in the sky, transforming the brisk morning chill into a wave of dry, relentless heat. Claire had layered up when she first stepped into the vineyard, shivering against the crisp air, but now her jacket was tied around her waist, and sweat trickled down her neck. The contrast was startling, and she wasn't sure what was more exhausting—the rapid change in temperature or the hours she'd spent bent over the vines.

Wiping her forehead with the back of her hand, she leaned against the post of a trellis to catch her breath. The heat radiated off the ground, and the scent of sun-warmed grapes mingled with the earthy tang of soil. Her muscles ached in places she hadn't thought about in years, but there was an odd satisfaction in the rhythm of the work—the snip of the clippers, the rustle of leaves, and the steady thud of grapes landing in the baskets.

Ethan appeared at the end of the row, carrying two bottles of water. His shirt was now damp with sweat, clinging to his shoulders in a way that emphasized how much time he spent outdoors. He handed her a bottle, his expression neutral but not unkind.

"Not bad for a city girl," he said, his voice carrying a hint of teasing.

Claire took the bottle and drank deeply, the cool water a welcome relief. "Don't sound so surprised," she said, wiping her mouth. "I can handle hard work."

Ethan smirked and leaned against the trellis. "I'm starting to see that. Most people quit after an hour."

"Is that why you invited me?" she asked, raising an eyebrow. "To see if I'd give up?"

"Maybe," he admitted, though his tone was more curious than accusatory. "But you're still here, so maybe I underestimated you."

Claire set the bottle down and glanced out over the vineyard. The lake sparkled in the distance, and the soft hum of activity surrounded them. "I can see why you love this place," she said after a moment. "It feels… timeless."

Ethan followed her gaze, his expression softening. "It's home. Always has been."

She studied him, her curiosity getting the better of her. "What about before this? Did you ever want to leave? Go somewhere else?"

He shook his head. "Not really. There's something about this land—once it's in your blood, it's hard to imagine being anywhere else."

Claire nodded, feeling the weight of his words. She envied his connection to this place, the sense of purpose that seemed to ground him.

"You're different from what I expected," he said suddenly, his eyes meeting hers.

Claire tilted her head. "What did you expect?"

Ethan hesitated, then shrugged. "Someone who'd show up, take a few pictures, write a surface-level piece, and move on."

"Well, sorry to disappoint," she said, her voice light but her gaze steady. "I'm not really into surface-level anything."

For a moment, they stood in companionable silence, the sounds of the vineyard filling the space between them. Then Ethan straightened and gestured toward the end of the row.

"Come on," he said. "There's something I want to show you."

Curious, Claire followed him through the vines and up a slight incline to a small clearing. A single, gnarled tree stood in the center, its twisted branches heavy with leaves. Beneath it was a weathered wooden bench, its edges smoothed by time and use.

"My grandparents used to sit here after every harvest," Ethan explained, his voice quieter now. "It was their spot. They'd bring a bottle of wine, talk about the season, and plan for the next."

Claire approached the bench and ran her hand along its surface, feeling the grooves and imperfections. "It's beautiful," she said softly.

"It's more than that," Ethan said, stepping beside her. "It's a reminder of why we do this. It's not just about the wine—it's about the people, the memories, the stories that get passed down."

Claire glanced at him, struck by the vulnerability in his tone. For the first time, she saw a glimpse of the man behind the guarded exterior—a man deeply connected to his roots, fiercely protective of his family's legacy.

"Thank you for sharing this with me," she said, her voice sincere.

Ethan nodded, his gaze lingering on hers for a moment longer than necessary. "You should get going," he said finally, breaking the spell. "There are other places you need to see, and we've got the rest of the harvest to finish."

Claire smiled, a mix of gratitude and something she couldn't quite name filling her chest. "I'll be back," she said as she started down the path.

Ethan watched her go, his expression unreadable.

Chapter 5

Claire took off the scarf around her neck as she stepped into the Okanagan Wine & Orchard Museum, located inside the Laurel Packinghouse, shaking off the crisp morning air that clung to her skin. The space smelled faintly of wood and fruit, a warm contrast to the sharp, earthy chill outside. The museum wasn't large, but it was beautifully curated—a tribute to the valley's rich agricultural history and its rise as one of Canada's premier wine regions.

She strolled past displays of vintage tools and photographs of early orchardists, her notepad tucked under one arm. Each artifact seemed to tell a story, from the sun-drenched fields of the first settlers to the sleek, modern wineries that now dotted the landscape. A guide explained the evolution of winemaking in the valley, her passion evident in every word.

"This is what I've been missing," Claire murmured to herself, scribbling notes. The museum was more than an introduction—it was a doorway into the heart of the Okanagan, and she couldn't wait to step through.

Claire's next stop of the day was **Sandhill Wines**, previously called Colona Wines, conveniently located just a short walk from the museum. The sleek, contemporary design of the tasting room was a stark contrast to the rustic charm she'd come to associate with vineyards, but it immediately set a tone of refinement. Sunlight streamed through floor-to-ceiling windows, casting a warm glow on the polished countertops and the bottles neatly arranged like art pieces on display.

Claire paused at the entrance, letting the quiet hum of conversation and the faint clink of glasses wash over her. A friendly sommelier approached her with a welcoming smile.

"Welcome to Sandhill Wines," the sommelier said, offering her a glass of their signature Chardonnay to start the tasting.

Claire took the glass, swirling the wine carefully before taking a sip. The bright, crisp flavor surprised her—hints of green apple and citrus, balanced by a subtle creaminess. "Wow," she murmured.

The sommelier smiled knowingly. "That's from our Sandhill Estate Vineyard, where the unique terroir gives it that lively acidity. We focus on single-vineyard wines to highlight the characteristics of each site."

As Claire moved through the tasting flight, she learned how Sandhill collaborated with local growers across the Okanagan, sourcing grapes from distinct microclimates to craft wines that were as varied as the land itself. A Merlot from their Phantom Creek Vineyard carried deep, rich notes of plum and cocoa, while the Syrah from King Family Vineyard had a bold peppery finish that lingered on her palate.

The sommelier gestured toward a map on the wall, marked with the locations of the vineyards Sandhill sourced from. "Each site has its own story, its own personality. Our job is to let that shine through in every bottle."

Claire scribbled notes furiously in her notebook, captivated by the depth of knowledge and passion poured into each explanation. As she savored a final sip of their Small Lots Viognier, she couldn't help but marvel at how much this one winery had already taught her about the Okanagan's winemaking diversity.

Before she left, she paused outside, glancing back at the sleek tasting room and the rows of vines stretching toward the horizon. The day had only just begun, but already she felt as though she was uncovering something profound—not just about the region, but about the people who poured their hearts into these wines.

Claire's next stop took her to **The Vibrant Vine**, a winery just a short drive from downtown that promised a completely different experience.

From the moment she pulled into the parking lot, Claire could tell this was no ordinary winery. A riot of color greeted her— murals splashed across the walls, a painted piano perched on the patio, and whimsical sculptures scattered throughout the property.

Inside the tasting room, the artistic flair was even more pronounced. Every wall was covered in bold, psychedelic designs that seemed to ripple and shift with the light. One of the staff members greeted her with a cheerful smile and handed her a pair of 3D glasses.

"You'll want these," they said, winking. "Everything here is meant to be seen in another dimension."

Claire slipped on the glasses, and the already vibrant artwork came alive, layers of depth and motion leaping from the walls. She couldn't help but laugh softly at the sheer playfulness of it all.

"This place is incredible," she said, taking in the surreal scene.

The staff guided her to the tasting bar, where the first pour was their signature Woops White blend. Claire lifted the glass, taking in the wine's pale golden hue before swirling and sipping. Bright notes of pear and citrus danced across her tongue, balanced by a crisp, clean finish.

"This is fantastic," Claire said, jotting notes in her book. "What's the story behind the name?"

The sommelier chuckled. "Legend has it that the first batch of this wine was a happy accident—an unexpected mix-up in the winemaking process. It turned out so well that we decided to keep it, and Woops White was born."

Claire smiled, charmed by the story. As she sampled a few more wines, including a bold Cabernet Sauvignon and a refreshing Pinot Gris, she couldn't help but marvel at the blend of creativity and craftsmanship that defined The Vibrant Vine.

Before leaving, she took a moment to wander through the outdoor art installations, her notebook in hand. The entire experience felt less like a winery visit and more like stepping into a dream—one where art, wine, and imagination collided in the best possible way.

Claire's third stop brought her to **Tantalus Vineyards,** a place she'd been particularly eager to visit.

The drive up the hill was lined with rows of vines that seemed to stretch endlessly toward the horizon, framing a breathtaking view of Okanagan Lake glimmering in the distance. When she stepped out of her car, the serene atmosphere hit her immediately. The quiet hum of nature paired with the expansive view felt like stepping into a painting.

Inside the tasting room, Claire was greeted by a staff member who exuded warmth and enthusiasm. "Welcome to Tantalus Vineyards," they said, pouring her a small sample of their flagship Riesling.

Claire hesitated for a moment before raising the glass to her nose. She'd promised herself not to overindulge—tasting five wineries in one day required more discipline than she'd anticipated. Setting the glass down after a careful sip, she discreetly used the spittoon provided, a habit she had quickly adopted after her second stop.

The sommelier smiled, seemingly used to this from more seasoned wine tasters. "Good call. You're pacing yourself like a pro."

Claire chuckled. "It's harder than it looks. But this Riesling—wow. It's so vibrant."

The sommelier nodded. "It's what we're known for. Tantalus is one of the oldest continuously producing vineyards in British Columbia. Our Riesling vines date back decades, and everything we produce is made from estate-grown grapes. It's a commitment to sustainability and quality."

Claire took another small taste, letting the crisp acidity and delicate notes of green apple and lime linger on her palate. She scribbled in her notebook, jotting down phrases like bright minerality and pure expression of heritage.

"What makes this vineyard so unique?" she asked, looking out at the rows of vines through the large windows that framed the lake below.

The sommelier followed her gaze. "It's the location, the age of our vines, and our dedication to sustainable practices. The Okanagan Valley's climate gives us warm days and cool nights, perfect for Riesling. And because we use only estate-grown grapes, we can control every step of the process—from the vineyard to the bottle."

Claire nodded, impressed. There was a clarity in Tantalus's approach that mirrored the wine itself—nothing extraneous, just the purity of the land and the skill of those who cultivated it.

After tasting a Pinot Noir with a silken texture and a Chardonnay with a hint of stone fruit, Claire stepped outside to the terrace. She let her eyes wander over the panoramic view of the vineyard, with Okanagan Lake shimmering in the midday sun.

She jotted a few more notes: A place where the past and future meet, rooted in tradition but always evolving.

Before she left, the sommelier handed her a bottle of their Riesling as a gift. "Something to remember us by," they said with a smile.

Claire thanked them, tucking the bottle carefully into her bag. She was learning that every winery had its own story, its own personality—and Tantalus was no exception. As she drove away, she couldn't help but think that there was something poetic about the way the land, the vines, and the people all worked together to create something so timeless.

Chapter 6

Claire's fourth stop brought her to **Sperling Vineyards**, a place steeped in history and family tradition.

The moment she arrived, Claire could feel the difference. Unlike the polished modernity of some of the other wineries she had visited, Sperling exuded a quiet charm that spoke to its roots. Nestled among gently sloping hills, the winery was surrounded by neatly tended rows of vines that seemed to stretch endlessly toward the horizon.

As she stepped out of her car, she was greeted by the winery's owner, a warm and welcoming woman who introduced herself as Ann.

"Sperling Vineyards has been in my family for nearly a century," Ann said as they began to walk through the vineyard. "My grandparents started it in 1925. Back then, this wasn't wine country—it was orchard country. They were true pioneers."

Claire listened, captivated, as Ann explained how the family had transitioned from growing fruit to cultivating grapes, always with an eye toward sustainability. "We've been practicing organic and biodynamic farming for years," Ann said, pausing to touch a leaf on one of the vines. "It's about more than just growing grapes. It's about creating balance—respecting the land so it can keep giving back."

They stopped at a block of vines marked with a small wooden sign: Old Vines Foch, Planted 1968.

"These are some of the oldest vines in the Okanagan," Ann said, her voice tinged with pride. "Old vines give the wine a unique complexity—you can taste the years in every glass."

Back in the rustic tasting room, Claire sampled their Old Vines Foch Reserve. The deep, inky wine carried notes of dark fruit, leather, and spice, with a richness that lingered long after she'd tasted it.

"This is remarkable," Claire said, jotting notes in her notebook. "There's so much depth to it."

Ann smiled. "It's a labor of love. Old vines don't produce as much fruit, but what they do give us is unparalleled. It's like distilling the essence of the land itself."

As they talked, Ann shared stories of the vineyard's evolution—how each generation had contributed something new, from replanting vines to adopting biodynamic practices. For Claire, it was more than a history lesson. It was a testament to resilience, innovation, and the enduring power of family.

Before she left, Claire wandered through the small gift shop, pausing to admire old photographs on the walls. One in particular caught her eye—a black-and-white image of Ann's grandparents, standing proudly in front of their first harvest.

It struck her then how much of winemaking was about time—not just the time it took for grapes to ripen or for wine to age, but the time spent building something lasting, something worth passing down.

As she walked back to her car, a bottle of Old Vines Foch tucked safely in her bag, Claire felt a deep appreciation for the legacy of Sperling Vineyards. It wasn't just about the wine—it was about the stories rooted in every vine and every bottle.

Claire's final stop of the day took her to **Kitsch Wines**, a boutique winery perched on a hill with sweeping views of the Okanagan Valley.

As she pulled into the driveway, the sleek, modern aesthetic of the winery stood in stark contrast to the rustic charm of the day's earlier stops. A bright, airy tasting room greeted her, its large windows framing the vineyard and the glistening waters of Okanagan Lake below.

Claire paused for a moment outside, taking in the view. The sun hung low in the sky, casting a golden glow over the vines, while the lake shimmered in the distance. It was almost too beautiful to be real, and she knew this would be the perfect spot to end her day.

Inside, the vibe was decidedly youthful and energetic. Music played softly in the background, and the staff moved with an easy confidence that matched the winery's sleek design. A cheerful host handed Claire a glass of their signature Pinot Noir Rosé as she approached the tasting bar.

"Our Rosé is estate-grown," the host explained, gesturing toward the rows of vines visible through the windows. "We focus on small-batch production to really showcase the quality of the grapes and the care that goes into every bottle."

Claire lifted the glass to her nose, inhaling the vibrant aroma of fresh strawberries and citrus. She took a small sip, letting the crisp, refreshing flavors dance across her palate. "It's so bright and lively," she said, jotting notes in her journal.

"That's what we aim for," the host said with a grin. "Kitsch is all about celebrating the fun side of wine without compromising on quality. We like to think of ourselves as approachable but still serious about what we do."

As she moved through the tasting flight, Claire couldn't help but admire the balance the winery had struck between playfulness and professionalism. From the cheeky labels on their bottles to the thoughtful craftsmanship of the wine itself, every detail seemed to reflect the winery's personality.

"You know," she said, setting down her glass of Chardonnay, "This feels different from the other places I've visited today. There's something… youthful about it."

The host laughed. "That's exactly what we're going for. We're not trying to be the biggest or the oldest—we're just trying to make great wine and have a little fun while we're at it."

Claire spent a few more minutes soaking in the atmosphere, chatting with the staff and jotting down observations. As she stepped outside to take in the view one last time, she reflected on how each winery she'd visited had its own unique character.

Some, like Tantalus and Sperling, were deeply rooted in tradition, with decades of history shaping their approach. Others, like Kitsch, embraced a modern energy that felt fresh and innovative. Together, they painted a picture of a region that was as diverse as it was passionate.

Back at her accommodation, Claire set down her notebook, now bursting with stories, flavors, and impressions. The Okanagan wasn't just a place—it was a tapestry woven from the land, the people, and the wines they created. And as she thought about the journey ahead, she felt a surge of excitement to share this world with her readers.

Chapter 7

The rhythmic pulse of live music spilled into the cool night air as Claire stepped through the doors of the Blue Gator Club. Inside, the room was alive with energy—dim lighting, the hum of conversation, and the steady thrum of bass that vibrated through the floorboards. She'd stumbled across the place while wandering downtown, drawn in by the sound of a local band warming up and the promise of unwinding after a long day of winery tours.

Claire slid onto a barstool, her notebook left behind for the night. This wasn't about work; this was about soaking in the local vibe and letting herself enjoy the moment. She ordered a glass of wine—something light and familiar—and turned her attention to the stage as the band launched into a lively blues number.

"Didn't expect to see you here," came a voice beside her.

She turned, surprised to find Ethan leaning casually against the bar, a beer in hand. He was dressed down—jeans, a well-worn T-shirt, and that ever-present air of quiet confidence.

"Ethan," she said, her lips curving into a smile. "What are you doing here?"

"Could ask you the same thing," he said, his tone teasing. "Didn't peg you for a live blues kind of girl."

Claire raised an eyebrow. "And what kind of girl did you peg me for?"

He smirked, taking a sip of his beer. "The type who spends her nights buried in a notebook, dissecting the 'natural characteristics' of Pinot Noir."

Claire laughed, the sound surprising even herself. "Fair enough. But even I need a break from all the wine talk now and then."

He gestured to the stool beside her, and when she nodded, he slid onto it. For a moment, they sat in comfortable silence, the music filling the space between them.

"How's the article coming?" Ethan asked, turning his attention back to her.

"It's... coming," Claire said, swirling the wine in her glass. "Today was a whirlwind. Five wineries, each one completely different.

It's a lot to take in, but I think I'm starting to get a feel for the valley."

"Let me guess," Ethan said, his lips quirking into a half-smile. "You've got your favorites already."

Claire tilted her head, her eyes narrowing playfully. "And if I do?"

"I'll just have to hope mine's on the list," he said, his tone light but his gaze steady.

She held his gaze for a beat longer than she intended, feeling a flicker of something unspoken pass between them. "I think you'll be happy with what I've written so far," she said finally.

"Good to know," Ethan replied, leaning back slightly. "So, what stood out the most today?"

Claire thought for a moment, her fingers tracing the rim of her glass. "It's hard to say. Each place had its own personality, its own story. But the one thing they all have in common is how much heart goes into what they do. You can feel it in the wine, in the way they talk about the land. It's... inspiring."

Ethan nodded, his expression thoughtful. "That's what makes this place special. It's not just about the wine—it's about the connection to the land, the people. You don't get that everywhere."

Claire smiled, the warmth of his words settling over her like a blanket. "You really love it here, don't you?"

"Yeah," he said simply. "I do."

For a moment, the noise of the bar seemed to fade, and it was just the two of them. Claire took another sip of her wine, trying to ignore the way her pulse quickened under his steady gaze.

"You should visit my vineyard again," Ethan said, breaking the silence. "We're pressing grapes later this week. It's messy, but it's something worth seeing."

"I might take you up on that," Claire said, her lips curving into a slow smile. "If you're willing to give me another tour, that is."

"Deal," Ethan said, tipping his beer toward her.

The band launched into a raucous rendition of an old classic, and Claire laughed as Ethan leaned closer, his voice low so she could hear him over the music. "Think you can handle another day in the dirt?"

"I think I'm tougher than you give me credit for," she said, her tone playful.

He grinned, and for the first time, Claire saw something in his expression—a spark of mischief, of interest—that sent a thrill through her.

As the night wore on, their conversation ebbed and flowed, punctuated by laughter and the occasional shared look that felt charged with possibilities. When they finally parted ways, Claire couldn't help but feel that this night had shifted something between them—something she wasn't quite ready to name but couldn't deny.

Chapter 8

Claire woke with the first rays of sunlight peeking through the curtains of her small bed-and-breakfast room. The coolness of the early morning air drifted through the slightly cracked window, a quiet reminder of how unpredictable the Okanagan temperatures could be. Deciding she needed to stretch her legs before the day's winery visits, she slipped on her jacket and headed out for a walk.

City Park was nearly deserted at this hour, the calm serenity of the space a welcome change from the hum of activity she'd encountered the previous night at the Blue Gator Club. The gentle lap of waves against the shore of Okanagan Lake was the only sound, punctuated by the occasional call of a bird in the distance. Claire breathed deeply, the crisp air filling her lungs as she wandered along the winding paths.

Near the water spray park, her attention was drawn to a group of children climbing on a larger than life concrete statue of three bears, their laughter carrying in the breeze. Claire stopped to watch them, smiling at their boundless energy despite the chill in the air. She found a bench nearby and sat down, letting the warmth of the rising sun slowly warm her fingers.

"You'd think it was the middle of summer with how they're playing," a woman's voice said, drawing Claire's attention. She turned to see a couple sitting on the next bench, sipping from steaming travel mugs.

Claire chuckled. "Kids have a knack for ignoring the cold, don't they? I'm Claire, by the way."

The couple introduced themselves as locals—Mark and Jenna—parents of two of the children racing through the now closed for the season spray park. Before long, they fell into easy conversation, and it didn't take long for the topic to turn to the lake.

"So, have you seen the Ogopogo yet?" Mark asked, grinning.

Claire tilted her head, intrigued. "Ogopogo?"

Jenna nodded enthusiastically. "It's our very own lake monster. Legend has it that it's been here for centuries—long before the settlers arrived. The Indigenous stories describe it as a water spirit, but over time, it's become something of a local mascot."

Mark leaned forward, his tone conspiratorial. "You'll hear all kinds of stories from people who swear they've seen it. Long neck, humps in the water, that sort of thing. Some even claim it's a relative of the Loch Ness monster."

Claire laughed, imagining a mysterious creature lurking beneath the tranquil surface of Okanagan Lake. "And do you believe in it?"

Jenna shrugged, her smile warm. "I think it's part of what makes this place special. Whether it's real or not, Ogopogo keeps the imagination alive, and it connects us to the stories of the past."

Mark gestured toward the lake, now glowing under the early morning light. "It's funny—people come here for the wine and the scenery, but it's things like Ogopogo that make them stay. This valley has a way of getting under your skin."

Claire looked out at the lake, the water sparkling like liquid gold in the sunlight. She could see what they meant. There was something about this place—a mix of beauty, history, and a hint of the unknown—that felt larger than life.

"Thank you for sharing that," she said, jotting a note in her pocket journal. "It's… enchanting."

As the children called out for their parents, Claire waved goodbye to the couple and began to make her way back toward the bed-and-breakfast. The day ahead promised more winery visits, but for now, she savored the quiet magic of the valley. Ogopogo, or no Ogopogo, this place had already begun to weave its spell on her.

Chapter 9

The café buzzed faintly with the hum of quiet conversations and the occasional clink of a coffee cup against a saucer. Claire sat by the window, her laptop open but untouched, the cursor blinking impatiently on a blank document. Her latte had gone cold, the foam collapsed into a thin, unappealing film. It mirrored how she felt—deflated, unsure, and teetering on the edge of irrelevance.

She stared at the screen, willing herself to write something—anything. But the words wouldn't come, just as they hadn't for months. Her memoir, *Chasing Shadows*, had been meant to be her magnum opus, the deeply personal project that would elevate her from a competent journalist to a respected author.

Instead, it had landed with a thud.

Her publisher's polite but clinical feedback still rang in her ears: "It's well-written, Claire, but it's missing heart. Readers won't connect with a collection of events. They need to feel what you felt, to understand why these stories matter to you."

The words had stung, not because they were harsh, but because they were true. Claire had poured months of work into the memoir, but somewhere along the way, she'd held back. She'd hidden behind polished prose and carefully crafted anecdotes, too afraid to reveal the raw vulnerability that made those moments real.

She'd avoided writing about the breakup with Adam, the relationship that had unraveled in her hands while she was too focused on chasing deadlines to notice the fraying edges. She'd skimmed over her mother's illness, touching lightly on hospital visits but never delving into the sleepless nights, the helplessness of watching someone you love slip away piece by piece.

Instead, Chasing Shadows had become exactly what her publisher said it was—a collection of well-written but distant stories.

When the reviews came in, they'd been lukewarm at best. Critics praised her technical skill but lamented the lack of emotional depth. "Cerebral but cold," one particularly scathing review had read. Sales had been equally disheartening. The memoir had quickly sunk to the bottom of the publisher's priorities, overtaken by newer, flashier releases.

Claire rubbed her temples, trying to dispel the ache that had taken up permanent residence there since the book's rejection. She'd wanted so badly for it to succeed—not just for the accolades or the sales, but to prove to herself that she could be more than a journalist-for-hire. That her voice mattered.

The Kelowna assignment had been her last chance, a way to claw her way back to relevance. Her editor, Marcy, had framed it as an opportunity, but Claire wasn't naïve. She knew it was a test. If she couldn't deliver something extraordinary, she might not get another assignment at all.

Her thoughts drifted back to Toronto, to the tiny apartment where she'd written her first published article by the dim light of a desk lamp that barely worked. Back then, she'd written with a fire in her belly, driven by the need to prove herself. She missed that version of herself—the one who hadn't yet been bruised by rejection and the creeping fear that maybe her best work was behind her.

A waitress approached, clearing away her untouched latte. "Can I get you another?"

Claire shook her head, forcing a smile. "No, thanks. I should probably get going."

The truth was, she didn't know where to go. The vineyards, the lake, the mountains—they were all stunning, but they only made her feel more like an outsider, a Vancouver city girl who didn't belong in a place so steeped in tradition and history.

She packed up her laptop and stepped outside, the fresh air biting her cheeks. The streets were quieter now, the small-town charm of Kelowna a stark contrast to the relentless pace of Toronto and Vancouver.

As she walked aimlessly, her thoughts looped back to Marcy's instructions, *Make it personal, Claire. Something that matters.*

The irony wasn't lost on her. She was in a place brimming with stories, but the one she couldn't seem to write was her own.

For the first time since arriving, she let herself feel the weight of it all—the rejection of her memoir, the gnawing self-doubt, and the pressure of proving she was still capable of telling a story worth reading.

The air was crisp, carrying the faint scent of pine and distant smoke. Claire stopped on a small bridge near the Delta Grand Okanagan Resort overlooking a pond, the water slightly flowing beneath her. It reminded her of something her mother used to say, "Rivers don't fight the rocks in their path. They flow around them, reshaping themselves as they go."

She took a deep breath, letting the words settle over her. Maybe she couldn't fix everything—not her memoir, not her past— but she could still move forward, reshaping herself as she went.

With that thought, Claire turned back toward the B&B, her steps a little steadier than before. The vineyard tours could wait until tomorrow. Tonight, she needed to sit down and confront the blank page again—not for Marcy, not for her career, but for herself.

She wasn't done yet. Not by a long shot.

Chapter 10

After a refreshing morning walk through City Park, where the cool air had left a rosy glow on her cheeks, Claire returned to the bed-and-breakfast with a sense of quiet anticipation for the day ahead. She grabbed her notebook, packed her camera, and set off on the short drive to **St. Hubertus & Oak Bay Estate Winery**.

The road curved gently through the valley, flanked by orchards and glimpses of the sparkling lake. As she approached the winery, the gentle slopes of the vineyard came into view, their neatly arranged rows of vines glowing vibrant green in the morning sun. Against the serene backdrop of Okanagan Lake, the winery seemed to blend effortlessly into the landscape, exuding a sense of timelessness and tradition.

Stepping out of her car, Claire immediately felt the history of the place. Unlike some of the more polished, modern wineries she had visited, St. Hubertus exuded an old-world charm, its buildings understated yet welcoming, nestled harmoniously among the vines.

A cheerful staff member greeted her with a warm smile, handing her a glass of their Pinot Blanc to sip as they began the tour.

"This vineyard has been around since 1928," her guide explained as they walked along the gravel path toward the vines. "It's one of the oldest in the valley, and our family has been tending it for generations. We're proud to use sustainable farming practices and focus entirely on estate-grown grapes."

Claire nodded, taking a small sip from her glass before discreetly using the spittoon provided. She was determined to keep a clear head for the rest of the day. The Pinot Blanc was light and floral, with a crispness that mirrored the cool morning air.

"What's your most unique wine?" Claire asked, her curiosity piqued.

"That would be our Chasselas," the guide replied, leading her to a block of vines marked with a small wooden sign. "It's a white grape originally from Switzerland, and it's pretty rare around here. We've been growing it for decades, and it's a bit of a signature for us."

Back in the tasting room, Claire was handed a glass of Chasselas, its pale gold color catching the sunlight streaming through the windows. She inhaled the delicate aroma before tasting it—subtle notes of apple and pear with a smooth, almost creamy finish.

"This is incredible," she said, jotting notes in her journal. "It's so gentle but full of character. I've never tasted anything quite like it."

"That's what we love about Chasselas," the guide said, beaming. "It's unassuming but versatile. It pairs beautifully with almost anything, and it really reflects the unique qualities of our vineyard."

Claire spent another hour exploring the property, learning about their winemaking process and their efforts to preserve the land. She admired how the family's connection to the vineyard seemed woven into every aspect of their work.

Before leaving, she paused by the edge of the vineyard, gazing out over the lake. The breeze carried the faint scent of grapes, mingling with the earthy aroma of the soil. It was a moment of quiet reflection, the kind that seemed to happen more often in this valley.

"This place is special," she murmured to herself as she snapped a photo of the vines.

With a bottle of Chasselas carefully tucked into her bag, another gift, Claire climbed back into her car, ready for the next stop on her itinerary. The day was still young, and the Okanagan had more stories to reveal.

Claire's next stop was **CedarCreek Estate Winery,** a place she'd heard about for its reputation as a leader in sustainable winemaking.

Nestled on the eastern shores of Okanagan Lake, the winery's elegant yet understated design seemed to echo its philosophy—respect for the land paired with a commitment to quality. The drive along the lake had been nothing short of breathtaking, with the sparkling water glistening under the mid-morning sun, and now, standing at the entrance to CedarCreek, Claire felt a renewed sense of curiosity for what lay ahead.

Inside, the modern tasting room was warm and inviting, with floor-to-ceiling windows offering panoramic views of the vineyards and lake beyond. A sommelier greeted Claire and led her to a quiet corner of the room where a flight of their Platinum series wines awaited.

"We'll start with the Chardonnay," the sommelier said, pouring the pale golden wine into her glass. "This is one of our flagship wines, made entirely from estate-grown grapes."

Claire lifted the glass to her nose, inhaling the delicate aroma of stone fruit and subtle oak. Taking a small sip, she savored the wine's bright acidity, balanced by a creamy texture and hints of peach and apricot.

"It's so well-rounded," Claire said, jotting notes in her notebook.

"That's the magic of the Okanagan," the sommelier replied with a smile. "The climate here gives us warm days and cool nights, which is perfect for growing grapes with vibrant flavors and natural balance."

Next was the Pinot Noir, a deep ruby-red wine that immediately caught Claire's eye. She swirled the glass, watching the legs slowly slide down the sides before taking a sip. The flavors unfolded gradually—cherry and raspberry at first, followed by earthy undertones and a hint of spice.

"It's complex," Claire said, thoughtfully. "There's a lot going on here."

"Pinot Noir is known as the 'heartbreak grape,'" the sommelier explained. "It's notoriously difficult to grow, but when it works, it's worth the effort. This one is a great example of what our vineyard can produce when we nurture it properly."

Between pours, the sommelier shared stories about CedarCreek's history, including its transition to organic farming and the meticulous care taken to ensure sustainability at every step. Claire was particularly fascinated by the winery's commitment to preserving biodiversity, from using cover crops to encourage beneficial insects to planting native flora around the vineyard.

"Wine is more than what's in the glass," the sommelier said, pouring the final wine of the flight, a bold Syrah. "It's about the connection between the land, the people, and the process. That's what we try to honor here."

Claire nodded, appreciating the sentiment as she tasted the Syrah. It was rich and velvety, with notes of blackberry, pepper, and a whisper of smoke—a fitting end to the flight.

After the tasting, she stepped out onto the terrace, where the view of the lake stretched endlessly before her. She let the breeze carry away the last traces of the wine, grounding herself in the moment.

Looking out at the lake and the surrounding vineyards, Claire couldn't help but reflect on how each winery she visited seemed to embody a distinct personality, yet as she noted before, all shared a profound respect for the valley and its potential.

With a notebook full of impressions and a newfound admiration for the artistry of winemaking, Claire thanked the staff and made her way back to her car. One more stop awaited her today, and she was ready to end her journey on a high note.

Chapter 11

Claire's final destination for the day was one she had been anticipating since the beginning of her journey. Perched on a gentle slope overlooking Okanagan Lake, **Summerhill Pyramid Winery** was impossible to miss, its gleaming white pyramid standing tall agmonst the backdrop of lush green trees.

She parked her car and lingered for a moment, marveling at a view that never seemed to lose its charm. The air seemed different here—lighter, almost charged. The pyramid stood like a sentinel, its symmetry both striking and mysterious, as if it held secrets of the universe within its geometric walls.

Inside the tasting room, Claire was greeted with a warm smile and a glass of their sparkling Cipes Brut, an organic wine that danced on her palate with its delicate bubbles and citrus notes. She moved through the flight of wines, savoring the crisp minerality of the Riesling and the bold, earthy character of their Syrah. Each sip reflected the winery's deep commitment to organic and biodynamic practices, a philosophy that also supports their renown as one of British Columbia's largest producers of Icewine.

"The secret," her guide explained as they walked toward the pyramid, "Is how we treat the land—and what happens in the pyramid."

Claire raised an eyebrow. "The pyramid? It's not just for storage?"

The guide smiled knowingly. "It's far more than that. You'll see."

The tour began with an explanation of the winery's biodynamic methods—everything from planting and harvesting according to lunar cycles to composting with natural materials to enrich the soil. Claire listened, intrigued, but it was when they entered the pyramid that her curiosity turned to awe.

Inside, the temperature dropped slightly, and the atmosphere shifted. The light filtered through narrow openings, casting soft, golden beams onto rows of wine barrels and bottles. The air smelled faintly of oak and aging grapes, a grounding contrast to the ethereal energy that seemed to hum through the space.

"Our wines are aged here," the guide said, gesturing to the barrels. "The pyramid's design is based on sacred geometry, aligned with the cardinal points and proportions found in the Great Pyramid of Egypt. We believe this space enhances the energy of the wine as it ages, balancing and harmonizing it."

Claire's skepticism wavered as the guide led her to a small, circular area in the center of the pyramid. Arranged around it were several crystal singing bowls, their translucent surfaces catching the light.

"We host group meditations here, each offering a unique experience," the guide explained, motioning for Claire to sit on a cushion. "Tonight's session will feature crystal bowls. Their vibrations resonate through the space, creating harmonic frequencies that infuse the wines—and those who join us— with balanced energy. Would you like to try it?"

Curiosity won out, and Claire nodded, settling herself on the cushion.

The guide began to play, gently running a mallet along the edge of one of the bowls. The sound that filled the space was otherworldly— pure, resonant, and deeply calming. The vibrations seemed to ripple through the air, sinking into Claire's chest and spreading warmth through her body.

She closed her eyes, letting the sound envelop her. It was as if the notes were unlocking something inside her, a quiet release of tension she hadn't even realized she was holding. The layers of sound built and shifted, creating a symphony of tones that seemed to echo not just in the pyramid but in the very core of her being.

When the last note faded into silence, Claire opened her eyes, blinking as if emerging from a dream. The space felt different now—lighter, almost luminous. She glanced at the barrels and bottles around her, imagining the wine inside absorbing the same vibrations she had just experienced.

"How do you feel?" the guide asked, her voice soft.

"Like I just woke up," Claire said, her own voice barely above a whisper. "It's... incredible."

The guide smiled. "That's the power of resonance. It's not just the wine that absorbs it—it's us, too. Energy is all around us. Here, we just help it along."

As Claire stepped out of the pyramid and back into the golden evening light, she felt a quiet reverence for what she had just experienced. It wasn't just about the wine or the meditation—it was about the connection to something larger, something unspoken but deeply felt.

Driving back to the bed-and-breakfast, Claire couldn't shake the feeling that today had been about more than research or wine tasting. It had been a reminder of the magic that could be found in unexpected places— and the way it could resonate long after the moment had passed.

Chapter 12

The morning arrived with a crisp chill in the air, the kind that hinted at the changing seasons while still promising the warmth of the sun later in the day. Claire found herself once again navigating the winding road to Ethan's vineyard, her excitement tempered by a touch of curiosity. She couldn't quite picture what "pressing grapes" entailed, but Ethan's words from the other night had stuck with her.

"It's messy, but it's something worth seeing."

As she pulled into the gravel driveway, the vineyard stretched before her, its rows of vines now bearing the signs of harvest—some stripped bare, others heavy with the last clusters of grapes waiting their turn. The landscape was alive with activity, workers moving purposefully between the vines and the barn.

Ethan emerged from the barn, his sleeves rolled up and his hands dusted with a faint purple hue. His expression softened when he saw her, and he waved her over.

"Right on time," he said, his tone teasing. "Ready to get your hands dirty?"

Claire smiled. "I thought I was just observing. You didn't mention a dress code for grape pressing."

He chuckled, gesturing to the apron draped over his arm. "You're lucky—I came prepared."

She followed him into the barn, where the earthy scent of grapes and fermenting wine filled the air. Large bins brimming with freshly picked grapes lined one side of the room, and the hum of machinery provided a steady background rhythm.

"This is where the magic starts," Ethan said, leading her to a sorting table. "We remove anything that shouldn't be here—leaves, stems, anything that could mess with the flavor."

Claire watched as workers deftly sorted through the grapes, their hands moving with practiced precision. Ethan handed her a small cluster.

"Try one," he said.

She plucked a grape from the bunch and popped it into her mouth. The sweetness was intense, with a hint of tartness that lingered on her tongue.

"Delicious," she said, reaching for another.

"Don't get too comfortable," Ethan said, grinning. "This is the easy part."

He led her to the pressing area, where the grapes were funneled into a large machine that gently crushed them, releasing their juice. Claire watched in fascination as the juice flowed into a tank, its color a rich, deep purple.

"It's incredible," she said, scribbling notes in her journal. "So much work goes into this stage alone."

Ethan nodded. "It's a process, but it's worth it. This is where the wine begins to take shape. Every decision we make here affects what ends up in the bottle."

As the morning wore on, Ethan guided her through the various steps, from fermentation tanks to barrel storage, explaining how each stage was carefully managed to bring out the best in the wine.

"What I love about this," Ethan said as they walked through the rows of barrels, "Is that it's always a collaboration. The land, the grapes, the people—they all have to work together. You can't rush it, and you can't force it. You just have to respect the process."

Claire glanced at him, struck by how his words seemed to mirror his approach to life.

After a brief break for lunch, Ethan invited her to join the workers in one final task—pressing the last bin of grapes for the day. Claire hesitated for only a moment before pulling on the apron he'd handed her earlier.

It was messy work, just as Ethan had warned, but there was something undeniably satisfying about it. The sticky sweetness of grape juice clung to her hands, the rhythmic sound of the press grounding her in the moment.

By the time the day ended, Claire was exhausted but exhilarated. As she stood in the barn, wiping her hands on a towel, Ethan handed her a glass of wine—freshly pressed juice that had only just begun its transformation.

"Here," he said, his tone softer now. "A taste of what's to come."

Claire raised her glass, taking a sip. It was raw and unpolished, but full of potential.

"It's amazing," she said, smiling.

"So are you," Ethan replied, his eyes meeting hers for a long, quiet moment.

For the first time, Claire didn't rush to fill the silence. Instead, she let it linger, the faint hum of the vineyard around them, the weight of the day's work settling into her bones.

As the sun dipped lower in the sky, casting a warm orange glow over the vineyard, Claire packed up her notes and thanked the workers who had shared their day with her. Ethan walked her to her car, his hands tucked casually into his pockets, his easy confidence softened by the weariness of the day's labor.

"So," he said, leaning against the car door as she opened it, "You survived your first grape press. Not bad for a city girl."

Claire laughed, brushing a stray lock of hair out of her face. "Not bad? I think I handled it like a pro."

He smirked. "Sure, but let's see how you handle what comes next."

She tilted her head, intrigued. "What comes next?"

Ethan pushed off the car, his gaze meeting hers. "How about a pint at O'Flannigan's? It's not as fancy as your wineries, but it's got character. And they pour the best Guinness this side of the Atlantic."

Claire hesitated, the idea of unwinding after such a full day suddenly appealing. "I don't know," she teased. "I might be too exhausted to keep up with you."

He grinned, a flicker of mischief lighting his expression. "Somehow, I think you'll manage."

For a moment, they stood there, the playful energy between them charged with something more. Then Claire nodded. "Alright, you're on. But if they don't have a decent cider, you're buying."

Ethan chuckled, opening her car door for her. "Deal. I'll see you there."

As she drove away, Claire couldn't help but smile, the prospect of the evening bringing a lightness to her that had nothing to do with her work. The vineyard, the wine, and now this—the Okanagan was beginning to feel like more than just a story. It was beginning to feel like something she wasn't ready to leave behind.

Chapter 13

Claire stepped into O'Flannigan's Pub, and the atmosphere hit her like a wave. The hum of voices, laughter, and clinking glasses filled the air, accompanied by the steady bass of a classic rock song blasting from the speakers. The place was packed with energy—groups of university students crowded around tables, playing card games and sharing pitchers of beer, while others gathered by the pool table, cheers erupting with every sunk shot.

She spotted Ethan near the bar, standing with an easy confidence that seemed to radiate from him. He wore a relaxed flannel shirt and jeans, blending effortlessly with the casual crowd. When he saw her, he lifted his pint in greeting, his smile disarmingly warm.

"You made it," he said as she approached.

Claire gave him a wry smile. "I wasn't going to miss out on the best Guinness in town, was I?"

He chuckled and gestured to the bartender. "What are you drinking?"

"Surprise me," she said, leaning against the bar.

Ethan raised an eyebrow but didn't question her. Moments later, the bartender slid a glass of cider her way. "Thought this might suit you better than a Guinness," Ethan said, smirking.

She took a sip, the crisp sweetness a refreshing change from the day's wine. "You're lucky—I like it."

They found a small table in the corner, away from the loudest groups but still close enough to soak in the pub's lively atmosphere. Ethan leaned back in his chair, his beer in hand, and watched as Claire took in the scene.

"Not exactly the vibe of a winery tasting room," he said, a hint of amusement in his tone.

Claire laughed. "That's putting it mildly. But I kind of like it. It's... unpolished."

"Like me?" he asked, his grin turning playful.

Claire tilted her head, pretending to consider. "Maybe a little."

Their laughter came easily, the conversation flowing as naturally as it had at the vineyard. They talked about everything from her impressions of the wineries she'd visited to Ethan's stories about growing up in the valley.

"So, what's the verdict?" Ethan asked, his gaze steady. "Is the Okanagan living up to your expectations?"

"It's more than I expected," Claire admitted, her tone softening. "There's so much heart here—so many stories. It's hard not to feel inspired."

He nodded, his expression thoughtful. "That's what keeps me here. It's not just the land or the wine—it's the people, the connections. That's what makes it all worth it."

For a moment, their eyes met, and the noise of the pub seemed to fade into the background. Claire felt the pull of something unspoken between them, a quiet understanding that didn't need words.

A burst of laughter from a nearby table broke the moment, and Claire took a sip of her cider to steady herself. "So," she said, leaning forward, "Do you come here often, or was this just an excuse to get me out for a drink?"

Ethan smirked, the flicker of mischief returning to his eyes. "Maybe a little of both."

They stayed until the crowd began to thin, their conversation ebbing and flowing like the rhythm of the music. When they finally stepped outside, the cool night air was a sharp contrast to the warmth of the pub.

"Thanks for coming," Ethan said, his voice quieter now. "It was nice to step away from everything for a bit."

Claire smiled. "I'll admit, I needed it too. Sometimes it's good to get a little... unpolished."

He walked her to her car, their steps unhurried. As she unlocked the door, she hesitated, looking at him for a moment longer than she meant to.

"See you at the vineyard?" she asked, her voice softer than before.

Ethan nodded, his expression unreadable but warm. "Yeah. See you."

As she drove away, the glow of the evening lingered, weaving itself into the fabric of her growing connection to the valley—and to Ethan.

Chapter 14

Over the next few days, Claire immersed herself in the rich tapestry of the Okanagan Valley's wine culture, visiting a variety of wineries and deepening her appreciation for the region's viticulture. Eager to explore further, she set her sights on Summerland, a charming town renowned for its picturesque vineyards and unique wine experiences.

As Claire drove along the lakeside highway, the shimmering expanse of Okanagan Lake stretched out to her left, reflecting the clear morning sky like a sheet of glass. The charming town of Peachland came into view, its lakeside cafes with inviting patios and the occasional kayaker gliding effortlessly across the tranquil waters. Just beyond Peachland, the road opened up to reveal a striking view of Rattlesnake Island—a rugged, rocky outcrop rising dramatically from the shimmering waters of Okanagan Lake. Claire slowed the car, her gaze drawn to the island she'd read about the night before. According to local legend, this small, unassuming landmass nestled within the boundaries of Okanagan Mountain Park was known as "Monster Island." The name stemmed from the myth of Ogopogo, the lake's fabled creature, said to dwell in a hidden cave beneath the island's jagged shores.

Seeing it now, its stark silhouette against the blue waters, Claire couldn't help but imagine the stories that had circulated for generations. The idea of a lake monster seemed almost whimsical, yet the island's rugged presence gave the legend a sense of possibility that sent a ripple of curiosity through her.

The road leading to **8th Generation Vineyard** felt like a gateway to history. Its understated charm felt like a natural extension of the land, the neatly tended vines bathed in the golden light of the late morning sun. Claire had read about the Schales family, whose winemaking roots stretched back eight generations to Rheinhessen, Germany, and she couldn't help but marvel at the idea of such a legacy being transplanted into the Okanagan Valley.

When the vineyard finally came into view, it was understated yet inviting, blending seamlessly with the surrounding landscape. Rows of vines stretched across gently sloping hills, basking in the warmth of the late morning sun. Unlike some of the larger, more polished wineries she had visited, 8th Generation exuded an intimate charm, as if the vineyard itself carried the quiet confidence of generations past.

Claire stepped out of her car and was greeted by Steffan, one of the family members who now managed the vineyard. He had an easygoing demeanor, his handshake firm but warm. "Welcome to 8th Generation," he said. "Let's show you what makes this place special."

As they walked through the vineyard, Steffan shared the family's story. "We started in Rheinhessen, Germany—my ancestors were making wine there long before any of us were born. When we came to Canada, it wasn't about starting over; it was about continuing what they had built, just in a new place. The Okanagan has been good to us. Its unique climate has let us honor those traditions while experimenting with new techniques."

They stopped by a cluster of vines heavy with fruit. "This is where our Riesling starts," Steffan said, plucking a single grape and handing it to Claire. She bit into it, the sweetness balanced perfectly with a hint of tartness.

"It's amazing how much you can taste already," she said, jotting a quick note in her journal.

"It's all in the balance," he replied. "And that's the goal in the bottle too."

In the tasting room, Claire was guided through a flight of wines, each one reflecting a combination of heritage and innovation. The Riesling was the centerpiece, its delicate balance of sweetness and acidity showcasing the family's expertise. As she swirled the glass, the aromas of green apple and citrus filled the air.

"It's bright but so elegant," Claire said after her first sip.

"That's what we aim for," Steffan said with a nod. "It's about honoring the grape and the land while adding our own touch."

She moved on to the Pinot Noir, with its velvety texture and hints of cherry and spice, and then to the Merlot, whose rich blackberry notes lingered pleasantly on her palate. Each wine told its own story, but together they spoke of a family deeply connected to both their roots and their future.

After the tasting, Claire strolled through the vineyard again, soaking in the peaceful atmosphere. The rows of vines seemed to stretch endlessly, their symmetry both calming and awe-inspiring. She paused to admire the view of the lake in the distance, her thoughts wandering to the generations of winemakers who had brought this place to life.

Before she left, Steffan handed her a bottle of their signature Riesling, a parting gift that felt like a piece of the family's story. "Take this with you," he said. "It's a taste of what eight generations can do."

Claire smiled, touched by the gesture. As she drove away, the bottle safely tucked in her bag, she couldn't help but feel that her visit to 8th Generation was about more than just wine. It was a window into a legacy—a reminder that behind every vineyard was a family, a history, and a future waiting to be written.

Chapter 15

The drive to **Thornhaven Estates Winery** took Claire up a winding hillside road that offered increasingly breathtaking views of the valley below. By the time she arrived, she was greeted with a vista that seemed to stretch endlessly—the vibrant greens of the vineyards merging with the shimmering blue of Okanagan Lake in the distance.

The winery itself was striking, its Mediterranean-inspired architecture a unique contrast to the rugged beauty of the surrounding landscape. Arched windows framed the scenery like paintings, and the warm earth-toned stucco walls radiated a rustic elegance. Thornhaven felt like a slice of southern Europe transplanted into the heart of the Okanagan Valley.

As Claire stepped out of her car, the gentle hum of bees flitting through lavender bushes reached her ears, mingling with the faint strains of music coming from the tasting patio. The air was rich with the scent of grapes ripening on the vine and the floral notes of nearby gardens.

"Welcome to Thornhaven," a cheerful voice called out. Claire turned to see a woman in a wide-brimmed hat approaching her, carrying two glasses of pale, golden wine. "I'm Rachel. Let's get you started with our Gewürztraminer—it's the perfect introduction to what we do here."

They walked together to the patio, where Rachel gestured for Claire to sit at a table overlooking the valley. Claire lifted the glass to her nose, inhaling the wine's vibrant aroma— floral and fruity with hints of lychee and rose.

"This is fantastic," Claire said after her first sip, the wine's crisp, refreshing finish lingering pleasantly.

Rachel smiled. "Gewürztraminer is one of our specialties. It thrives in this climate, and we take a lot of pride in bringing out its full potential. That balance of aromatics and acidity is what makes it so unique."

After savoring the Gewürztraminer, Rachel led Claire on a short tour of the winery, sharing its history along the way.

"Thornhaven was established in 1999 by the Fraser family. The location is perfect for growing a variety of grapes thanks to the hillside's natural drainage and sun exposure."

Inside the winery, Claire marveled at the attention to detail in the architecture, from the handcrafted wooden beams to the intricately tiled floors. Everything about Thornhaven seemed designed to create an atmosphere of warmth and welcome.

The tasting continued with their Syrah, a bold red wine that unfolded on Claire's palate with notes of black pepper, dark fruit, and a whisper of smoke. Then came the Pinot Noir, its silky texture and flavors of cherry and spice a testament to the craftsmanship behind it.

"Each wine has its own personality," Rachel said, pouring the final sample. "But they all share one thing—this place. The soil, the sun, the care that goes into every vine—it's all reflected in the bottle."

Claire couldn't help but agree. As she stood on the terrace, the late afternoon sun casting a golden glow over the valley, she felt a deep appreciation for the connection between the land and the wine. Thornhaven wasn't just a winery—it was an experience, one that celebrated the Okanagan's beauty and bounty.

Before leaving, Claire was graciously gifted a bottle of Gewürztraminer, a thoughtful gesture that she knew would allow her to savor its crisp elegance long after her journey had ended. As she drove away, the breathtaking views of the valley slowly receding in her rearview mirror, she couldn't help but feel that Thornhaven had left a lasting impression—not just on her palate, but on her spirit.

Chapter 16

Claire's final stop of the day was **Dirty Laundry Vineyard**, a name that had intrigued her ever since she'd seen it on her itinerary. As she drove onto the sunlit plateau where the winery was perched, the expansive views of the surrounding valley took her breath away. Rows of vines stretched toward the horizon, their vibrant green contrasting with the dusty, golden hills in the distance.

The moment she stepped out of her car, she could hear the faint strum of a guitar carried in the breeze. Live music echoed from the winery's patio, setting a lively, almost festival-like atmosphere.

"Welcome to Dirty Laundry!" a cheerful host greeted her as she approached the tasting room. "You're just in time for the afternoon set. We've got live music most days—it's kind of our thing."

The tasting room itself was unlike any Claire had visited before. Playful and whimsical, it was adorned with vintage laundry equipment, cheeky signage, and decor that paid homage to the winery's colorful history. As the host poured her first sample, a crisp Gewürztraminer, she couldn't resist asking about the name.

"Well," the host began with a grin, "Back in the late 1800s, this land was home to a laundromat. But it wasn't just for washing clothes—it also doubled as a brothel. Of course, everyone in town pretended they didn't know, but the rumors always swirled. So, when we started the winery, we thought, why not embrace the story? 'Dirty Laundry' was the perfect name to honor the history and keep things fun."

Claire laughed, charmed by the story. "That's incredible. It definitely makes this place stand out."

As she moved through the tasting flight, Claire sampled their award-winning Hush Blush, a delicate rosé crafted from a blend of Merlot, Pinot Noir, and Cabernet Franc. The wine was vibrant and fruity, with a crisp finish that made it dangerously drinkable.

"This is fantastic," Claire said, jotting a note in her journal. "How do you achieve such a unique flavor profile?"

"It's all about the saignée method," the host explained. "We bleed off some of the juice early in the winemaking process, which gives it that beautiful color and concentrated flavor. It's one of our best sellers, and for good reason."

After the tasting, Claire wandered onto the patio, where a local musician strummed a bluesy tune under a canopy of string lights. The space was filled with laughter and conversation, the lively energy making it feel more like a community gathering than a traditional winery. She took a seat with a glass of Hush Blush in hand, letting the music and the setting work their magic.

The vibe was relaxed yet refined, the perfect blend of sophistication and playfulness. Guests lounged in the sun, sharing charcuterie boards and swapping stories, while children played nearby in a small garden area. The winery's history might have been scandalous, but its present-day atmosphere was one of warmth and connection.

As the sun began to dip below the hills, casting a golden glow over the vineyard, Claire found herself reflecting on her day. From the deep-rooted traditions of 8th Generation Vineyard to the elegant serenity of Thornhaven Estates and now the whimsical charm of Dirty Laundry, each winery had offered its own unique window into the soul of Summerland's wine culture.

The diversity of the experiences reminded her why she had fallen in love with storytelling in the first place. Each stop, each sip, each conversation had added a new thread to the tapestry she was weaving, not just for her article, but for herself.

With her heart full and her notebook brimming with ideas, Claire gathered her things and thanked the staff. As she drove away, the music from the patio still echoing in her mind, she couldn't help but smile. Dirty Laundry had been more than a winery—it had been a reminder that the best stories often come from the places that dare to embrace their quirks and imperfections.

Chapter 17

The sun had barely risen, casting a soft lavender glow over the hills, when Claire's phone buzzed on the bedside table. Groaning, she reached for it, squinting at the screen. Her editor, Marcy.

Claire swiped to answer and sat up, her heart already racing. Calls this early usually meant trouble.

"Morning, Marcy," she said, trying to sound more alert than she felt.

"Claire, we need to talk about your deadline," Marcy said, her tone brisk and direct. "How's the article coming along?"

Claire rubbed her temples, glancing at her notebook, which lay open on the desk across the room, pages crammed with hastily scribbled observations and half-formed ideas.

"It's... coming together. I just need a little more time to flush out the angles."

"Claire, you've been in the Okanagan for over a week now," Marcy replied, her voice tinged with impatience. "You promised me something fresh, something compelling. Right now, all I've got is a bunch of notes about wineries. Where's the story?"

Claire bristled, feeling the familiar sting of Marcy's no-nonsense approach. "It's more than just notes. There's a depth to this place—its history, its people. I'm weaving it all together."

"I'm sure it's beautiful," Marcy interrupted, "But we're on a deadline. This piece isn't just a travel puff—it's meant to stand out, to hook readers. I need conflict, Claire. Tension. Something that grabs them and makes them care."

Claire felt her frustration bubbling to the surface. "You want me to manufacture drama in a place that thrives on harmony?"

Marcy sighed. "No, but every great story has a turning point. Find yours. Dig deeper. There's always more beneath the surface."

The line went quiet for a moment, and Claire could hear the faint hum of city traffic on Marcy's end.

"Look," Marcy said finally, her tone softening. "I know you've got it in you.

You've written pieces that made me cry, Claire. Don't let this one fizzle out. Call me when you've got something more concrete."

The call ended before Claire could respond. She set the phone down, staring out the window at the vineyard-covered hills. The beauty of the valley had captivated her, but Marcy's words planted a seed of doubt.

Conflict. Tension. What did Marcy expect her to find?

She flipped through her notebook, skimming her notes. The wines, the stories, the people—everything seemed harmonious, almost idyllic. Was that the problem? Did the Okanagan lack the edge her editor craved, or was she simply not looking hard enough?

A sudden thought hit her like a glass of cold water. Ethan.

The image of his vineyard flashed in her mind, the way he had spoken so passionately about preserving his family's legacy. He had mentioned struggles, financial pressures, the challenges of keeping the vineyard afloat in a competitive market. Could that be the thread Marcy wanted her to pull?

Claire hesitated, a pang of guilt twisting in her chest. Ethan had trusted her, opened up to her in small but meaningful ways. Turning his story into her conflict felt like a betrayal, but she couldn't ignore the possibility that it might also be the key to saving her article.

Determined to clear her head, she grabbed her notebook and headed out the door. The cool morning air bit at her cheeks as she walked toward the lake, the stillness of the water a stark contrast to the storm brewing inside her.

As she reached the shore, she flipped to a blank page in her notebook and began writing, letting her thoughts pour out unfiltered. If there was a story here, she needed to find it—not just for Marcy, but for herself.

And if that meant digging deeper, she would. But she wasn't sure yet if she was ready for the consequences of what she might uncover.

Chapter 18

The morning sun cast a golden hue over the Okanagan Valley as Claire navigated her car northward toward Lake Country. The serene beauty of the landscape stood in stark contrast to the turmoil of her thoughts. Marcy's words echoed in her mind, urging her to uncover the deeper stories beneath the valley's picturesque surface.

Her first destination was **50th Parallel Estate Winery**, a modern architectural marvel nestled amidst rolling vineyards. The winery's sleek design, with expansive glass walls, offered panoramic views of Okanagan Lake, creating a harmonious blend of contemporary aesthetics and natural beauty. Known for its exceptional Pinot Noir, 50th Parallel had quickly gained a reputation for producing wines that reflected the unique terroir of the region.

As Claire entered the tasting room, she was greeted by a sommelier who guided her through a selection of their signature wines. The Pinot Noir stood out with its complex layers of cherry, earth, and subtle spice, leaving a lasting impression on her palate. The sommelier shared insights into the winery's commitment to sustainable practices and their meticulous approach to viticulture, emphasizing the importance of harmony between the vineyard and its environment.

Next, Claire visited **Ex Nihilo Vineyards**, a boutique winery celebrated for its artistic approach to winemaking. The name, Latin for "out of nothing," reflected the owners' journey of transforming raw land into a thriving vineyard. The tasting room doubled as an art gallery, showcasing works from local artists, creating an ambiance where creativity and viticulture intertwined seamlessly.

The highlight of her tasting was the Merlot, a rich and velvety wine with notes of blackberry and cocoa, embodying the passion and artistry that Ex Nihilo poured into their creations. Engaging with the staff, Claire learned about the challenges and triumphs of establishing a winery from scratch, gaining a deeper appreciation for the dedication required to succeed in the competitive wine industry.

Her final stop was **Gray Monk Estate Winery**, one of British Columbia's oldest family-owned wineries. Established in 1972 by the Heiss family, Gray Monk was instrumental in introducing Pinot Gris to Canada, earning them the title of the country's first family of Pinot Gris. The winery's name, translating to "Gray Monk," paid homage to the grape's origins in Europe.

Perched on a gentle slope overlooking the lake, Gray Monk's tasting room exuded rustic charm, with wooden beams and large windows framing the picturesque landscape. Claire sampled their Odyssey White Brut, a sparkling wine that danced on her palate with vibrant acidity and delicate bubbles. The experience was elevated by the staff's stories of the winery's pioneering spirit and commitment to excellence over the decades.

As the day drew to a close, Claire found herself on the winery's terrace, gazing out at the sun setting over the lake. The tranquil scene contrasted with the unease she felt about her article. The wineries she visited showcased passion, innovation, and a deep connection to the land, but Marcy's demand for drama lingered in her thoughts.

Her mind wandered to Ethan and the candid conversations they'd shared about the pressures of sustaining a family-run vineyard. The weight of his words now seemed to carry the tension Marcy sought. But was it ethical to delve into his personal struggles for the sake of her story?

Lost in contemplation, Claire's phone buzzed, jolting her back to reality. A message from Ethan lit up the screen: "Hope your day in Lake Country was enlightening. Let's catch up soon."

Claire sighed, the decision looming over her. She had come to the Okanagan seeking stories of wine and culture, but now she stood at a crossroads, torn between professional ambition and personal integrity.

As the first stars appeared in the twilight sky, Claire resolved to confront the dilemma head-on. She would meet with Ethan, not just as a journalist seeking a story, but as a friend grappling with the complexities of truth and trust.

With a heavy heart and a determined mind, Claire made her way back to her accommodation, the path ahead uncertain but unavoidable.

Chapter 19

The morning arrived with a golden glow that spilled through the curtains of Claire's room, casting long shadows across her notebook, which lay open on the desk. The pages were filled with scattered observations and ideas, but none of it felt cohesive enough for her article. Marcy's words from their call haunted her thoughts as she sipped her coffee, staring out at the shimmering Okanagan Lake.

Kelowna, with its easy blend of natural beauty and vibrant culture, had already started to feel familiar. There was a rhythm to the city she was beginning to appreciate—the way the mornings were calm and serene, only to give way to bustling afternoons at the waterfront. From the peaceful trails of Knox Mountain to the lively patios lining Bernard Avenue,

Kelowna had a personality that was both inviting and layered.

Yet, Marcy wanted drama.

The drama that Claire wasn't sure existed— at least, not in the way her editor envisioned. The valley thrived on harmony, not conflict. But as her phone buzzed with a message from Ethan, she couldn't ignore the quiet tension building within her.

Ethan: *"Are you free later today? Would love to hear how your trip to Lake Country went. We're bottling at the vineyard. It's a good time to drop by if you're up for it."*

Her stomach tightened. Ethan's vineyard had become a place she looked forward to visiting, but with Marcy's pressure looming over her, she couldn't shake the feeling that her motives had shifted.

The drive to Ethan's vineyard was as stunning as always, with the winding roads framed by vineyards and the lake shimmering like a jewel under the midday sun. Yet, Claire's mind was a jumble of conflicting thoughts.

When she arrived, the hum of activity greeted her. Workers moved between the barn and the vines, the sound of machinery punctuated by laughter and the occasional shout. Ethan stood near the bottling area, sleeves rolled up, his hands moving deftly as he worked alongside his team.

"Claire!" he called out, his face breaking into a grin as she approached. "Right on time."

She smiled, the sight of him momentarily easing her nerves. "Looks like you've got your hands full."

"Always," he said, gesturing for her to follow him. "Come on, I'll show you how it's done."

She spent the next hour observing the bottling process, the rhythmic clinking of glass and the earthy scent of wine filling the air. Ethan explained each step with a mix of pride and humor, his passion for the craft evident in every word.

"You make it look easy," Claire said, watching as he sealed a bottle with precision.

Ethan chuckled. "It's anything but. Every decision we make here—from the vines to the bottle—has weight. One wrong move, and it all falls apart."

The words hung in the air, heavier than they should have been. Claire hesitated, then decided to take the plunge.

"Ethan," she began cautiously, "You've mentioned before that things aren't always easy here. I hope you don't mind me asking, but… what keeps you going?"

He set down the bottle he was holding and turned to her, his expression thoughtful. "What keeps me going? The land, the legacy, the people who count on this place. It's not just about me—it's about everyone who's poured their lives into this vineyard."

Claire nodded, her notebook weighing heavily in her bag. "Do you ever feel like it's too much? Like there's a price to all of this?"

Ethan's gaze sharpened, and for a moment, she thought he might call her out. But instead, he sighed. "Of course. There are nights I wonder if we'll make it to the next season. But you can't focus on the fear. You focus on what you love, what matters."

Her heart twisted at the honesty in his words. Marcy's demand for conflict felt trivial in the face of Ethan's quiet resilience.

"Why do you ask?" Ethan asked, his voice gentle but probing.

Claire hesitated, her grip tightening on her bag. "Just… thinking about the angle for my article. There's so much heart here, Ethan. People should know about it."

His eyes softened, but there was an edge of wariness in his expression. "I trust you, Claire. Don't make me regret it."

The words were simple but heavy, and Claire felt the weight of them long after she left the vineyard that afternoon.

As she drove back to downtown Kelowna, the city welcomed her with its lively hum. She passed by Prospera Place, where crowds were gathering for a concert, and the historic Laurel Packinghouse, a nod to the valley's agricultural roots. Kelowna was full of stories—some light, some heavy.

The question was, which one would she choose to tell?

Chapter 20

The evening air was cool, carrying the faint scent of pine and the unmistakable freshness of Okanagan Lake. Claire had parked her car near the downtown waterfront, drawn to the allure of Kelowna's lively boardwalk. The hum of activity surrounded her—families strolling, couples sharing quiet moments on benches, and street performers captivating small crowds with music and tricks.

But Claire's mind was miles away.

Ethan's words from earlier lingered like a stubborn echo: "I trust you, Claire. Don't make me regret it." She knew he meant it as a reassurance, but it felt more like a warning.

Her notebook was tucked under her arm, heavy with potential—Ethan's story, the wineries, the culture of the Okanagan Valley.

But was it the story Marcy wanted? Was it enough?

She found herself walking toward the Cactus Club Cafe on the waterfront, its terrace buzzing with chatter and clinking glasses. It wasn't just a restaurant; it was a meeting point for locals and tourists alike, a place where the vibrant energy of the city seemed to converge. Claire grabbed a seat near the edge of the patio, where she could see the lights of the William R. Bennett Bridge stretching across the lake like a necklace of stars.

As she stared out at the water, her phone buzzed on the table. It was Marcy again.

"Claire," Marcy said the moment she answered, her voice brisk. "I need an update. Where are we with this story?"

Claire hesitated, her eyes fixed on the bridge. "It's coming together. The wineries, the people—they're all incredible. There's so much depth here."

Marcy sighed audibly. "That's great, but depth doesn't sell on its own. I need something that hooks the reader, something real. Conflict, Claire. Give me something that makes this more than a love letter to wine country."

Claire's grip tightened on the phone. "You want conflict? Fine. How about a small family vineyard struggling to survive in a market dominated by bigger players? Or a winemaker balancing the demands of tradition and innovation while fighting off bankruptcy?"

"Now we're talking," Marcy said, her tone sharpening with interest. "What vineyard?"

The question hit Claire like a punch to the gut. Ethan's face flashed in her mind, the trust in his eyes as they worked side by side that afternoon.

"I haven't decided yet," she said quickly, her voice more defensive than she intended.

"Well, decide fast," Marcy replied. "We've got a deadline, and I need a draft on my desk by the end of the week. Don't waste this opportunity, Claire."

The call ended, leaving Claire staring at the phone in her hand. Around her, the chatter and laughter of the terrace continued, oblivious to the storm brewing inside her.

As the night deepened, Claire wandered back toward the boardwalk. The soft glow of the streetlights reflected off the lake, creating an almost magical atmosphere. She passed by Kelowna's iconic Sails sculpture, its elegant curves illuminated against the dark sky.

She stopped, staring out at the water, where a small boat drifted lazily under the lights of the bridge. The scene was so peaceful, so serene, that it felt like a betrayal to think of exposing the struggles hidden beneath the valley's beauty.

But Marcy was right—conflict made a story compelling. And Ethan's vineyard was compelling.

The sound of her name startled her. She turned to see Ethan walking toward her, his hands in his jacket pockets, his expression unreadable.

"Ethan?" she said, her voice catching. "What are you doing here?"

"Could ask you the same thing," he said, stopping a few feet away. "Needed a walk to clear my head. Looks like I'm not the only one."

Claire tried to smile, but it didn't reach her eyes. "I've got a lot on my mind."

Ethan studied her for a moment, then nodded toward a nearby bench. "Care to share? Or are you keeping this one close to the chest?"

She hesitated, then sat down, Ethan joining her. The quiet stretched between them, filled only by the gentle lapping of the lake against the shore.

"You trust me," she said finally, her voice barely above a whisper. "Why?"

Ethan tilted his head, caught off guard by the question. "Why not?"

"Because I'm a writer," she said, turning to face him. "Because the truth is messy, and I don't know if I can tell it without hurting someone."

Ethan's jaw tightened, but he didn't look away. "Claire, if you're asking me whether I'm okay with you telling my story, I guess that depends on how you tell it. If it's the truth, then fine. But if you're looking for something sensational…"

"I'm not," she interrupted, her voice firm. "That's not who I am."

Ethan studied her, his gaze steady and unflinching. "Then write what's real. But don't pretend there's no cost. Stories have power, Claire. Make sure it's worth it."

Claire opened her mouth to respond, but Ethan raised a hand, a mischievous glint in his eyes interrupting the heaviness of the moment.

"You know what?" he said, his tone shifting. "Let's take a break from all this serious stuff. Come with me to Chances Casino. I've got a poker game calling my name, and you could use a distraction."

Claire blinked, caught off guard. "Poker? At a casino?"

"Why not?" he said with a shrug, his easy grin breaking through the tension. "Sometimes you've got to let the chips fall where they may—literally. And besides, it's better than sitting here overthinking."

Despite herself, Claire laughed. "I heard about the game, poker."

"Even better," Ethan said, standing and extending a hand to her. "Beginner's luck is a real thing. Trust me."

Claire hesitated for a moment before taking his hand, allowing him to pull her to her feet. The weight of her thoughts didn't vanish entirely, but as they walked toward his truck, the idea of losing herself in something as simple as a poker game felt strangely liberating.

"I can't believe I'm doing this," she muttered as they climbed in.

Ethan chuckled, starting the engine. "Welcome to the Okanagan, Claire. Sometimes the best stories are the ones you don't see coming."

As they drove toward the casino, the lights of the city shimmering in the distance, Claire felt a flicker of something she hadn't felt in days—hope.

Chapter 21

The lights of Chances Casino gleamed in the crisp night air as Claire and Ethan walked through the entrance. The hum of slot machines and the buzz of excitement washed over Claire, a stark contrast to the introspection of earlier.

"This place has some history," Ethan said as they walked through the main floor. "Used to be a bingo hall before they turned it into a full casino. I remember coming here with my parents when I was a kid—well, waiting outside in the car while they played bingo."

Claire glanced around, trying to picture the transformation. "A bingo hall, huh? Seems like it's come a long way."

"Yeah," Ethan said with a grin. "Back then, it was all folding chairs and coffee-stained tables. Now it's all lights and poker tables. Progress, I guess."

They weaved through the bustling crowd, past rows of slot machines and the low chatter of blackjack tables.

"Upstairs," Ethan said, gesturing toward the staircase with a nod. "That's where the real action happens."

Claire followed him to the second floor, her eyes taking in the transformation. The poker room was sleek and modern, with five felt-topped tables arranged in a spacious layout beneath warm pendant lights. The air was quieter than the bustling casino floor below, but the atmosphere buzzed with focus and anticipation. Each table had its own cluster of players, their attention fixed on the cards and chips in front of them, their expressions a mix of calculation and calm.

Ethan led Claire toward the desk at the entrance, where the pit boss stood, a clipboard in hand, overseeing the evening's games.

Ethan leaned casually against the desk. "Two spots at a table, please," he said, pulling out his wallet.

The pit boss nodded, reaching for a tray of chips. "Standard three hundred to start?"

"That'll do," Ethan replied, glancing at Claire. "And I'll cover hers too."

Claire froze, a sharp protest bubbling up as Ethan handed over the money for his chips and reached for his wallet again.

"Whoa, whoa, hold on," Claire said, stepping forward. "I can cover my own chips, thanks."

Ethan raised an eyebrow, his expression skeptical. "You sure? It's not exactly a cheap game, and I figured…"

Claire cut him off with a playful but firm tone. "You figured what? That a travel writer can't afford a poker game? Don't worry about me—I've got this."

Ethan hesitated, then smirked as she handed over her own cash to the pit boss, who slid a matching stack of chips her way.

"Alright, Bennett," Ethan said as they walked toward the table. "But don't say I didn't warn you. This isn't a slot machine."

Claire rolled her eyes, suppressing a grin. "You're awfully confident for someone who hasn't seen me play yet."

Ethan waved to the dealer at a table near the corner, who nodded in acknowledgment. They took their seats, Claire settling in with a calm demeanor that betrayed nothing of her intentions.

"You know," Ethan said as he arranged his chips in neat stacks, "I thought I was being nice, covering your buy-in. Didn't realize I was signing up for a lesson in independence."

Claire chuckled, her eyes flicking briefly to the cards the dealer began to shuffle. "You were being nice. But you might want to hold onto that cash—you're going to need it when you start losing chips to me."

Ethan laughed, shaking his head. "Bold words, Bennett. Let's see if you can back them up."

As the first hand was dealt, Claire couldn't resist a small smile. She knew exactly what she was doing, and Ethan had no idea what he was in for.

Claire settled in, smoothing her hands over the green felt, a flicker of excitement sparking in her chest.

"You sure you're ready for this?" Ethan teased as the dealer shuffled the cards.

Claire arched an eyebrow, a smile tugging at her lips. "You might be surprised."

As the cards were dealt, Ethan leaned back in his chair, glancing around the table. "Poker's a lot like running a vineyard," he said, almost to himself.

Claire glanced at him, intrigued. "How so?"

"Well," Ethan began, picking up his cards, "It's all about reading the room. You've got to know when to hold back, when to take risks.

The vines don't tell you outright what they need, but if you pay attention—really pay attention—you start to see the signs."

Claire considered his words as she peeked at her own hand. Ace and king of spades. A strong start. She placed her bet casually, her demeanor calm and unreadable.

"Sometimes," Ethan continued, "You've got to bluff. Make people think you've got everything under control, even when you're one bad card away from folding. That's the wine business in a nutshell."

Claire raised an eyebrow, calling his bet. "And what happens when you can't bluff anymore?"

Ethan shrugged, a small smile playing on his lips. "Then you hope the cards turn in your favor. Or you get up and try again tomorrow."

The first round played out with Claire matching the others' bets, her expression composed. Ethan watched her closely, his brow furrowing slightly as she won the pot with a flush.

"Beginner's luck, huh?" he said, his tone laced with suspicion.

Claire smirked, stacking her chips. "Who said I was a beginner?"

Ethan laughed, shaking his head. "You did. Alright, Bennett. Let's see what you've got."

As the night wore on, Claire's skill became undeniable. She bluffed effortlessly, read the other players like open books, and won several hands with a calm confidence that left Ethan both impressed and mildly bewildered.

"You've been holding out on me," he said taking a break, leaning back in his chair.

Claire shrugged, sipping her water. "You never asked."

He chuckled, shaking his head. "Well, now I know not to underestimate you."

The conversation shifted back to poker as they rejoined the table. Ethan's analogies about poker and the wine business grew more vivid with each hand, his passion for both subjects shining through.

"You know what they say about the river card?" Ethan asked as the final round of the night began.

Claire shook her head, her focus still on her cards. "What's that?"

"It's the great equalizer," he said, his voice quiet but firm. "You can plan, you can strategize, but in the end, the river card decides everything. It's like the weather in winemaking—one late frost, and your whole season changes."

Claire nodded, feeling the weight of his words. It wasn't just about poker or wine. It was about life and the things beyond their control, the risks they took, and the resilience it required.

By the end of the night, Claire had amassed a respectable pile of chips, earning nods of respect from the other players. Ethan, for all his analogies, finished with fewer chips but no less enthusiasm.

As they left the casino, the cool night air felt refreshing against her skin. Claire glanced at Ethan, her earlier worries momentarily forgotten.

"You know," she said, her tone teasing, "You might be decent at poker if you didn't talk so much about wine."

Ethan laughed, the sound warm and genuine. "And you might be decent at wine if you didn't hustle people at poker."

They walked to the car, the lights of the casino glowing behind them. For the first time in days, Claire felt a little lighter, the drama of her article momentarily eclipsed by the simple joy of the night.

But as she climbed into the car, her thoughts drifted back to Ethan's words about the river card. The game wasn't over yet—not for her, not for him, and certainly not for the story she was trying to tell.

Chapter 22

$\mathcal{I}$t was another glorious fall day, with the sun casting a golden hue over the Okanagan Valley as Claire drove toward **Indigenous World Winery**. Located in West Kelowna, the winery was renowned for its seamless blend of modern viticulture and Indigenous heritage. Claire had heard of its unique approach and was eager to explore how the traditions of the Syilx people intertwined with contemporary winemaking.

Pulling into the parking lot, Claire's attention was immediately drawn to a striking teepee near the entrance. Adorned with vivid designs, the structure seemed to stand as both a guardian of the land and a powerful symbol of the Syilx people's enduring connection to it.

Stepping out of her car, Claire took a moment to take in the tranquil scene. The air carried the earthy scents of sage and pine, blending harmoniously with the understated elegance of the winery. The teepee wasn't just decorative—it was a statement of identity, a reminder of the harmony between history and modernity that defined Indigenous World Winery.

A friendly staff member approached, introducing herself as Maya. "Welcome to Indigenous World Winery," she said warmly. "Would you like to start with a tasting?"

"Yes, please," Claire replied, taking a seat at the polished bar.

Maya began pouring a selection of wines, each accompanied by stories of their origins. "This is our Hee-Hee-Tel-Kin White Blend," she explained, placing a glass in front of Claire. "The name means 'rare bird' in Nsyilxcən, the language of the Syilx people."

Claire took a sip, noting the crisp acidity balanced with floral notes. "It's delightful," she remarked. "How did the winery come to be?"

Maya smiled, clearly proud of the establishment's roots. "Robert and Bernice Louie, descendants of the Syilx people, founded the winery in 2016. Their vision was to merge modern winemaking with

Indigenous culture, honoring the land that their ancestors have protected for thousands of years."

As Claire continued the tasting, she couldn't help but admire the thoughtful integration of Indigenous heritage into every aspect of the winery. The labels featured animals significant to the Syilx people, such as the bald eagle and red fox, while the interior design showcased traditional art pieces.

"How has the community responded to the winery?" Claire inquired.

"The response has been overwhelmingly positive," Maya replied. "We've become a gathering place for both locals and visitors, offering a space to learn about Indigenous culture while enjoying quality wines. It's about creating a dialogue and fostering understanding."

After the tasting, Claire wandered through the gift shop, which offered handcrafted items from local Indigenous artisans. She selected a beautifully woven basket as a memento of her visit.

As she prepared to leave, Claire reflected on her experience. Indigenous World Winery wasn't just about producing exceptional wines; it was a celebration of heritage, resilience, and the deep-rooted connection between the Syilx people and the land. In her quest to uncover stories of conflict or controversy, she instead found a narrative of harmony and cultural pride.

Driving away, Claire felt a renewed sense of purpose. The Okanagan Valley held myriad stories, each unique and deserving of recognition. And sometimes, the most compelling tales were those of unity and shared history.

Chapter 23

The late afternoon sun dipped low in the sky, casting long shadows across Claire's desk at the B&B. Her notebook lay open, its pages filled with detailed observations and anecdotes from her visit to Indigenous World Winery. Yet, as she flipped through the pages, a gnawing sense of dissatisfaction settled in her chest.

She had been searching for conflict, something to satisfy Marcy's demand for tension, but all she had found was harmony and innovation. Ethan's struggles still lingered in the back of her mind, but she had resolved not to exploit his story. Yet, without it, her article felt incomplete.

Her phone buzzed, pulling her from her thoughts. A text from Marcy lit up the screen: "Update? I need something gripping, Claire."

Claire sighed, running a hand through her hair. She needed air, a distraction. Grabbing her jacket, she decided to take a walk down to the lakefront.

The boardwalk was lively despite the cooling evening air. Families strolled hand in hand, laughter and the occasional bark of a dog punctuating the gentle sound of waves lapping against the shore. Claire pulled her jacket tighter, her thoughts swirling.

The bright lights of Moo-Lix Ice Cream caught her attention as she walked along Bernard Avenue. A small line had formed outside, a mix of locals and tourists savoring their cones as they chatted or strolled past. The sweet aroma of freshly made waffle cones wafted through the air, and Claire's resolve to keep walking wavered.

She stepped inside, scanning the display of vibrant flavors until one caught her eye, lavender honey. The description promised a delicate floral sweetness with a smooth, creamy finish. Intrigued, she ordered a single scoop in a waffle cone.

The first taste was a revelation—the subtle earthiness of lavender balanced perfectly with the honey's natural sweetness. Claire found herself savoring each bite as she wandered back toward the boardwalk, the cold treat provided a sharper chill against the refreshing evening breeze.

As she neared the marina, her cone now half-eaten, a familiar figure caught her eye. Ethan stood near the edge of the dock, his phone pressed to his ear. Even from a distance, the tension in his posture was unmistakable.

Curiosity tugged at her, and she hesitated before stepping closer. Ethan's voice carried on the breeze, sharp and clipped, his usual calm nowhere to be found.

"I've told you before," he said, his back turned to her. "I'm not selling. I don't care what the offer is."

Claire froze, suddenly feeling like an intruder.

"You can't just waltz in and buy out generations of work," Ethan continued, his voice rising. "This isn't just a business to me. It's my family's legacy."

There was a pause, and Ethan let out a frustrated sigh, his free hand raking through his hair.

"No, I don't need more time to think about it. The answer's the same. It's always going to be no."

He ended the call abruptly, shoving his phone into his pocket. As he turned, his eyes met Claire's, and his expression shifted from anger to surprise.

"Claire," he said, his voice softer now, but still strained. "What are you doing here?"

"I was just taking a walk," she said quickly, stepping closer. "I didn't mean to eavesdrop, but… is everything okay?"

Ethan hesitated, the fight draining from his shoulders. "It's nothing. Just business."

Claire tilted her head, her brow furrowing. "That didn't sound like 'nothing.'"

He sighed, leaning against the dock's railing. "It's a developer. They've been trying to buy the vineyard for months now. Throwing around big numbers like it's going to make me forget what the place means."

"Why do they want it?" she asked, genuinely curious.

"Land," he said simply. "They don't care about the vines or the wine. They see the property as prime real estate for some resort or luxury homes. But I'm not selling."

Claire nodded, her heart sinking at the thought. She could see why Ethan was so protective of the vineyard—it wasn't just his livelihood, it was his identity, his connection to his family's history.

"Have you told anyone else about this?" she asked.

"Just my sister," he admitted. "But I didn't want to worry her. She's got enough on her plate."

They stood in silence for a moment, the weight of the conversation settling between them.

"Ethan," Claire said cautiously, "This could be the story I've been looking for. But I'd only write it if you're okay with it. Your side, your words."

His eyes met hers, a flicker of vulnerability breaking through his guarded expression. "And what happens if I say no?"

"Then I'll keep looking," she said firmly. "I'm not here to exploit you, Ethan. I'm here to tell the truth. But only if you want it told."

He studied her for a long moment, the tension in his jaw easing slightly. "Let me think about it," he said finally.

Claire nodded, understanding the weight of what he was considering. As they walked back toward the boardwalk together, the soft glow of the city lights reflecting off the water, Claire felt the tide shifting. Drama had found its way into her story—not through conflict she had sought, but through the truth she had stumbled upon.

Chapter 24

Claire sat on the veranda of the B&B, a steaming cup of coffee cradled in her hands. The morning sun filtered through the trees, casting dappled light across the wooden deck. In the distance, the vineyards stretched toward the lake, the rows of green catching the soft breeze. It was a quiet moment, one she'd rarely allowed herself in the past few years.

Her thoughts drifted, unbidden, to her life back in Vancouver, the city she called home now but rarely felt settled in. The pace of the bustling streets, the endless grind of deadlines, and the towering skyline often left her feeling boxed in. Vancouver's beauty—its mountains, ocean, and rain-kissed air—was undeniable, but it often felt like a backdrop to a life she wasn't fully living.

Before Vancouver, there was Toronto. She had grown up in the sprawling metropolis, where life moved at a relentless speed. Toronto was where she'd learned the value of hard work, where she'd carved out her identity as a writer. It was where she'd experienced her first taste of independence, but also where she'd felt the sting of heartbreak and failure.

She took a sip of her coffee, letting the warmth ground her as she compared the frenetic energy of the city to the unhurried rhythm of the Okanagan Valley. Here, life seemed to flow differently. The people she'd met—winemakers, families, locals—spoke in tones that suggested a deep connection to the land, as though time itself moved in step with the changing seasons.

It was a stark contrast to the life she'd built, chasing stories and deadlines, constantly moving but never quite arriving. In Toronto, the winters were long and biting, the summers humid and thick with the smell of asphalt. In Vancouver, it rained more often than not, the grey skies sometimes a mirror of her own mood.

But here in Kelowna, the air was different—lighter, more open. The mornings carried the scent of pine and ripening fruit, and the evenings were filled with the golden light of sunsets that lingered on the horizon.

Claire wondered what it would be like to live here, to trade the rush of the city for the steadiness of the valley. Could she let go of the constant need to prove herself? Could she find the same kind of peace that seemed to come so naturally to people like Ethan?

Her phone buzzed on the small table beside her, pulling her out of her thoughts. It was a text from Marcy: "Claire, we need to finalize the angle. Call me when you can."

The tug of the city, its demands and expectations, was relentless. Claire sighed, setting the phone face down. For now, she wanted to hold onto this moment, to reflect on the choices that had brought her here and the possibilities that lay ahead.

Looking out at the vineyards, she felt a small pang of longing—not just for the simplicity of this place, but for something she hadn't yet been able to name.

Chapter 25

The late morning sun poured through the open doors of the vineyard's tasting room, bathing the space in golden light. Claire walked in, greeted by the inviting aroma of oak barrels and the faint tang of fermenting wine. Ethan stood near a long counter, a row of glasses in front of him filled with varying shades of ruby red and amber gold.

"Right on time," Ethan said, glancing up as she entered.

"Am I interrupting?" Claire asked, taking in the orderly chaos of the space.

"Not at all," Ethan said with a smile. "You're just in time for the best part— blending."

Claire raised an eyebrow as she approached. "Blending? You do that too. Funny, I always thought wine came from a single type of grape."

Ethan chuckled, shaking his head. "Sometimes. But most wines are blends—different varietals combined to create balance and complexity. It's like cooking. You don't just throw in one spice and call it a day."

He gestured to the glasses. "Take these, for example. Each one is from a single varietal we grow here. On their own, they're fine. But together…" He picked up a glass and swirled it, the deep red liquid catching the light. "Together, they can be something special."

Intrigued, Claire stepped closer, watching as Ethan carefully measured wine from one glass into another. "Is this part of the process standard, or do you just go by feel?"

"A little of both," Ethan said. "There's science to it, of course—acidity, tannins, aromatics. But at the end of the day, it's about intuition. Knowing when to push boundaries and when to hold back."

He handed her one of the glasses. "Here, try this."

Claire lifted the glass, inhaling deeply before taking a sip. The flavors unfolded in layers—bright fruit notes at first, followed by a velvety smoothness that lingered.

"Wow," she said, her eyes widening. "That's incredible."

Ethan smiled, clearly pleased. "Now, compare it to this." He handed her another glass, this one slightly darker in color.

She sipped again, noting the stark difference. This wine was bolder, with an earthy undertone that seemed to ground it.

"They're so different," she said, glancing between the two glasses.

"Exactly," Ethan said. "Each varietal brings something unique to the table. The art is in finding the right balance."

Claire nodded thoughtfully, setting the glass down. "It sounds like life, doesn't it? Trying to figure out how to balance all the pieces."

Ethan's smile softened. "It is. You can't rush it, either. Sometimes it takes years to get it right. And even then, you're always learning."

They continued tasting and blending, Ethan explaining the nuances of each varietal and how it contributed to the final product. Claire found herself drawn not just to the process but to the passion in Ethan's voice as he spoke.

"So, what's your favorite part of all this?" she asked as they finished another round of blending.

Ethan paused, leaning against the counter. "This part, actually. The blending. It's when everything comes together. It's when you see the potential, the possibilities. It's not just about making wine—it's about creating something that tells a story."

Claire smiled, his words resonating deeply. "I think I get that."

Ethan glanced at her, his expression curious. "What about you? What's your favorite part of writing?"

Claire hesitated, the question catching her off guard. "I think it's similar, actually," she said after a moment. "Finding the right balance—between fact and feeling, between what's said and what's left unsaid. It's about creating something that connects with people."

Ethan nodded, his gaze steady. "Then I guess we're not so different, you and I."

Claire felt a warmth rise in her chest at his words. They stood in comfortable silence for a moment, the clinking of glasses and the hum of the vineyard filling the space around them.

As they returned to the task at hand, Claire couldn't help but feel that the act of blending wasn't just about wine—it was about finding harmony, not just in the glass, but in life itself.

Chapter 26

The late afternoon sun cast a golden glow over the vineyard as Ethan finished tidying up the blending station. He glanced over at Claire, who was scribbling furiously in her notebook, her brow furrowed in concentration.

"Hey," he said, leaning casually against the counter.

Claire looked up, her pen hovering mid-air. "What's up?"

"How do you feel about dinner tonight?" he asked, his tone light but inviting.

"Dinner?" she repeated, closing her notebook.

"Yeah. There's a place I think you'd like—Freddy's Brew Pub. It's got great food, their own craft beers, and some local history I think you'll find interesting."

Claire smiled, intrigued. "Alright. I'm in. But only if you promise I don't have to talk about the article for one night."

Ethan laughed. "Deal. But I'm warning you—there's also bowling."

Freddy's Brew Pub was bustling with the hum of conversations and the clinking of glasses as they walked in. The air carried the aroma of wood-fired pizza and freshly brewed beer, and the warm, welcoming atmosphere immediately put Claire at ease.

"Freddy's has been a Kelowna staple for years," Ethan explained as they were seated in a cozy booth. "It's attached to McCurdy Bowling Centre. Back in the day, it was themed around Fred Flintstone—you know, 'Freddy's.' They've modernized a bit since then, but the name stuck."

Claire looked around, noticing the subtle nods to its history in the playful decor and vintage bowling memorabilia displayed on the walls. "That's such a fun story. And they brew their own beer?"

"Yep," Ethan said, gesturing to the menu. "Their craft beers are excellent. You've got to try the Big Red Ale—it's one of their specialties."

Taking his suggestion, Claire ordered the ale while Ethan opted for their Lager. Their meals arrived shortly after, and they dove into plates of crispy chicken wings and wood-fired pizza, the flavors rich and satisfying.

"This is amazing," Claire said between bites. "And the beer is perfect with it. Do they make everything in-house?"

"Pretty much," Ethan said. "The owner is all about local ingredients and keeping it unique. It's one of my favorite spots to unwind."

After dinner, Ethan leaned back in his chair, a sly grin spreading across his face. "You ready to hit the lanes?"

Claire groaned, laughing. "You're serious about the bowling, aren't you?"

"Absolutely," he said, standing and offering her a hand. "Come on, it'll be fun."

The bowling alley was alive with energy—bright lights, the sound of pins crashing, and bursts of laughter from nearby lanes. Claire laced up her rented bowling shoes, already feeling out of her depth.

"I should warn you," she said, picking up a ball and testing its weight, "I'm terrible at this."

Ethan smirked, selecting his own ball with ease. "Good to know. I'll go easy on you."

She rolled her eyes but smiled, stepping up to the lane. Her first attempt sent the ball veering directly into the gutter, prompting a burst of laughter from both of them.

"Okay," Ethan said, stepping up behind her, "Here's a tip. Keep your wrist straight and aim for the arrows on the lane."

Claire nodded, determined to improve. Her second attempt wasn't much better, but she managed to knock down a single pin.

Ethan, on the other hand, bowled with effortless precision, sending the ball smoothly down the lane and landing a strike on his first try.

"Show-off," Claire teased as he turned back to her, grinning.

The game continued, with Claire's scores barely climbing while Ethan remained consistent. But the playful banter and shared laughter made her forget her embarrassment.

By the end of the night, Claire had managed a few spares and one lucky strike, which Ethan graciously applauded as though she'd won the game.

As they returned their shoes and prepared to leave, Claire looked at him with a smile. "Thanks for tonight. I really needed this."

Ethan's expression softened. "Anytime. You're not bad company, even if you're a terrible bowler."

Claire laughed, bumping his shoulder as they walked out into the cool night air.

Chapter 27

The morning sun filtered through the blinds in Claire's room at the B&B, but the warmth did little to ease the uneasy feeling gnawing at her. Last night at Freddy's had been the most carefree she'd felt in weeks, yet now, as the stillness of the morning settled in, the weight of unfinished decisions returned.

Her phone buzzed on the nightstand, breaking the quiet. It was Marcy. Claire stared at the screen for a moment before answering.

"Morning," she said, her voice still groggy.

"Morning? It's almost noon where I am," Marcy replied, her tone clipped. "Look, Claire, I need to know where we stand. Have you found the angle for the article? The clock's ticking."

Claire pinched the bridge of her nose, closing her eyes. "I'm working on it, Marcy.

I've got some really strong material. I just need more time to shape it."

"Time is a luxury we don't have," Marcy snapped. "The magazine needs something fresh and compelling, not another puff piece about wineries and sunsets."

Claire's stomach sank. "It's not a puff piece. There's depth here, real stories about the people who keep this valley alive."

"Good," Marcy said, her tone softening slightly. "Then find the conflict. Every good story has one, Claire. You're too good a writer to settle for fluff."

Before Claire could respond, the line went dead. She set the phone down, a knot forming in her chest. Conflict. She knew where it was—Ethan's battle with the developers trying to buy his land—but she also knew the cost of turning his struggles into a headline.

Later that day, Claire found herself back at the vineyard, notebook in hand, but her usual enthusiasm was absent. Ethan was in the middle of overseeing a delivery of new barrels, his easygoing demeanor intact despite the flurry of activity around him.

"You look like you didn't sleep," he said when he noticed her.

"Rough morning," Claire admitted, leaning against a stack of crates. "Marcy called. She's pushing me to find more tension for the article."

Ethan's brow furrowed. "Tension? What does that even mean?"

"It means she wants conflict," Claire said, her voice heavy. "And I think she expects me to find it here."

Ethan's expression darkened. "Here, as in me?"

Claire hesitated, not wanting to confirm it but unable to deny it. "She doesn't know about…everything you're dealing with. But if she did…"

"She'd want you to exploit it," Ethan finished for her, his tone sharp.

"No," Claire said quickly. "I would never—Ethan, I haven't written a word about you or the vineyard without your consent, and I won't. But I can't lie—I'm torn. Your story…it could help people understand what it takes to keep a place like this alive."

Ethan stared at her for a long moment, the easy camaraderie of the past few days replaced by a guarded tension. "You don't get it, do you? This isn't just a story to me. It's my life. My family's legacy. I've spent years trying to protect it, and one wrong move—one article that paints the wrong picture—could ruin everything."

Claire felt the sting of his words, but she refused to back down. "I do get it, Ethan. That's why I've been so careful. I don't want to hurt you or this place. But don't you see? Your fight is important. People need to know about the pressures on small vineyards, about the developers trying to erase what makes this valley special."

Ethan shook his head, stepping back. "And what happens when the developers see the article? When they use it as leverage to make me look weak? Do you have an answer for that?"

Claire opened her mouth but found no words. The truth was, she didn't have an answer.

Ethan sighed, his frustration giving way to something closer to resignation. "I need to think, Claire. About all of this. About us."

The weight of his last words hit her harder than she expected. "Ethan…"

He raised a hand, stopping her. "Not now. I've got work to do."

Claire drove away from the vineyard with a heavy heart, her thoughts spinning. She knew the stakes—for Ethan, for her career, for the fragile connection they had built. And for the first time since arriving in the Okanagan, she wasn't sure if she could find the balance between telling the truth and protecting what mattered most.

As the road curved along the shimmering lake, she glanced at her notebook on the passenger seat. It felt heavier than ever, filled with stories waiting to be told but carrying the weight of impossible choices.

Chapter 28

The road wound upward, cutting through the dense forests of the Monashee Mountains. Claire's car climbed steadily, the lake and vineyards of the valley falling away behind her. As the elevation increased, the air grew crisper, and the horizon widened to reveal breathtaking views of rocky peaks and endless greenery.

Big White Ski Resort had been a spur-of-the-moment decision, a need to escape the tangled emotions of the last few days. Though the ski runs were quiet in anticipation of the coming snow, the village retained its charm, with its alpine-inspired architecture and a peaceful stillness that hinted at the flurry of activity it would soon see. The crisp air carried the faint promise of winter, and Claire felt a sense of calm as she walked through the quiet streets.

Claire strolled toward the village, her footsteps soft against the stillness of the mountain air. Snowshoe Sam's, a rustic pub and café known for its cozy atmosphere, beckoned with its warm glow.

Inside, the air was rich with the scent of chocolate and freshly brewed coffee. Claire ordered a hot chocolate, its steam curling upward from a generous topping of whipped cream. She found a seat by the window, the vast expanse of the mountains stretching out before her, and pulled out her notebook.

The title for her article had been eluding her for weeks, but now, with the tranquility of the mountains surrounding her, something clicked. She jotted down a rough idea:

"Vines and Valleys: The Resilient Heart of the Okanagan"

Claire paused, the pen hovering over the page. The title felt right—a nod to the land, the people, and the struggle she had come to understand. She took a deep breath and began to write.

Draft Excerpt:
The Okanagan Valley is a land of contrasts. Its sun-drenched vineyards and serene lakefronts speak of tranquility and abundance, yet

beneath the surface lies a story of resilience and determination. From the Syilx people who first nurtured this land to the winemakers who toil through the seasons, the valley thrives on the strength of those who call it home.

Ethan's vineyard is a microcosm of this spirit. Nestled in the rolling hills overlooking Okanagan Lake, it is a place where history, tradition, and innovation converge. But like many small vineyards, it faces mounting pressures—from the demands of modern winemaking to the looming threats of development.

Claire stopped, rereading the lines. The words felt heavy, charged with the weight of Ethan's story and the delicate balance she was trying to maintain.

Her mind wandered back to their conversation, to the frustration in his voice and the fear she had seen in his eyes. She didn't blame him for his hesitation. Writing this story wasn't just about capturing the beauty of the valley—it was about doing justice to the people who poured their lives into its soil.

The warm sweetness of the hot chocolate grounded her as she stared out the window. The mountains stood tall and unyielding, a reminder of the resilience she was trying to capture in her article.

She continued to write…

Chapter 29

Claire finished the last sip of her hot chocolate, savoring the comforting warmth it brought to her thoughts. Snowshoe Sam's had provided a quiet refuge, but the weight of her article and her conflicted emotions about Ethan lingered. She tucked her notebook back into her bag and decided to stretch her legs before heading back to Kelowna.

The village was tranquil, the kind of quiet that only came in the off-season. As she wandered along the dirt paths, she noticed a small shop tucked away at the edge of the main square. Its sign read, Heritage of the Hills: Local History & Artifacts.

Curiosity piqued, Claire pushed open the heavy wooden door. A small bell jingled, announcing her arrival. The shop was cozy and dimly lit, with shelves lined with books, photographs, and carefully labeled artifacts. The air carried the faint scent of old wood and history.

"Welcome," an older man said from behind the counter. He was tall and thin, his gray hair tied back in a loose ponytail. "Looking for something specific?"

"Just browsing," Claire said, her eyes scanning the room. "I'm a writer. I thought I'd stop in and see if there's anything interesting about the area."

The man nodded, his sharp eyes studying her. "We've got plenty of stories here. You'd be surprised how much history these hills hold."

As Claire wandered the aisles, a black-and-white photograph caught her eye. It showed a group of people standing in a vineyard, their faces weathered but proud. At the center stood a man holding a basket of grapes, his expression stoic.

"That's from the early days of winemaking in the valley," the man said, stepping up beside her. "The vineyard in that photo doesn't exist anymore. It was sold off, piece by piece, to developers decades ago."

Claire's stomach twisted. "What happened?"

"The family couldn't keep up with the pressures," he said, his tone matter-of-fact. "Back then, small vineyards didn't stand a chance against the big players. It's a shame, really. That land had some of the best soil in the valley."

The words hit Claire harder than she expected. The photo was a haunting reminder of the fragility of the life Ethan was fighting to preserve.

"I'm writing about the wineries in the Okanagan," Claire said, her voice quiet. "About the challenges they face."

The man gave her a thoughtful look. "It's a story worth telling, but it's not an easy one. People come here and see the beauty, the wine, the lifestyle—but they don't see the sacrifices behind it."

Claire nodded, feeling the weight of his words. As she turned to leave, the man handed her a slim book titled *Vineyards of the Past: Forgotten Stories of the Okanagan.*

"Take this," he said. "It might give you some perspective."

"Thank you," Claire said, clutching the book.

As she walked back to her car, her mind raced. The story she was writing wasn't just about Ethan or the valley—it was about the people who had come before, the legacies lost to time, and the resilience it took to endure.

Opening the book in the driver's seat, Claire flipped through its pages. The stories were raw and unpolished, but they carried a truth she couldn't ignore. Her article wasn't just about the vineyards—it was about the heart of the valley and the people who gave it life.

The drive down from Big White felt different. The beauty of the landscape was still there, but now it carried a deeper meaning. Claire's story had shifted, and with it, her understanding of what she needed to write— and what she was willing to fight for.

Chapter 30

The Okanagan Regional Library's Kelowna branch stood as a modern beacon of knowledge in the heart of downtown. Its sleek architecture and expansive glass windows invited natural light to flood the space, creating a warm and welcoming atmosphere. Claire stepped through the doors, her mind buzzing with questions sparked by her visit to the mountains.

Inside, the scent of books and the soft hum of hushed conversations greeted her. Rows of neatly arranged shelves stretched out like a labyrinth, and the large windows offered glimpses of Ellis Street bustling with life outside.

She approached the information desk, where a friendly librarian looked up with a smile.

"Hi, I'm looking to research the history of vineyards in the Okanagan Valley," Claire said, setting her bag on the counter.

The librarian nodded knowingly. "We have a local history section upstairs. You'll find books, maps, and even some archived newspapers. Let me show you."

Claire followed the librarian to an open staircase that led to the second floor. The local history section was tucked into a quiet corner, its shelves brimming with treasures from the past.

"This is where we keep most of our regional archives," the librarian said, gesturing to a microfilm reader nearby. "You'll find old articles, property records, and even personal accounts. Let me know if you need help."

"Thank you," Claire said, already scanning the shelves.

She started with a book titled Wine and Legacy: The Early Vineyards of the Okanagan. Its faded cover hinted at countless readings over the years. Sitting at a nearby table, Claire flipped through the pages, stopping at a section about the valley's first vineyards.

The names were familiar, but many of the stories were not. Some vineyards thrived through the decades, while others had succumbed to financial pressures, family disputes, or the lure of development. She jotted down notes, her mind painting a picture of the valley's complex past.

Curiosity led her to the microfilm reader, where she loaded an old reel of newspapers from the 1970s.

Headlines jumped out at her:

- *"Family Vineyard Closes Amid Rising Costs"*
- *"Developers Acquire Historic Okanagan Land"*
- *"Small Growers Face Challenges in Competitive Market"*

One article in particular caught her attention. It told the story of a vineyard much like Ethan's—family-owned, steeped in tradition, but ultimately sold to developers. The words felt eerily prophetic, echoing Ethan's fears.

Claire leaned back in her chair, staring at the screen. The story wasn't just about the vineyards that had been lost—it was about the people behind them. Families who had poured their hearts into the land, only to watch it slip away.

She reached into her bag for the slim book the man at the mountain shop had given her. Its pages now felt like pieces of a puzzle she hadn't realized she was assembling.

Claire glanced around the library, the quiet enveloping her like a cocoon. She opened her notebook and began sketching out a new direction for her article:

"Preserving the Roots: The Fragile Legacy of the Okanagan's Vineyards"

She scribbled notes furiously, ideas pouring out as she pieced together a narrative that wove the past with the present. Ethan's vineyard was part of this story, but so were the countless others that had fought to survive.

By the time Claire left the library, the sun was beginning to dip, casting a golden glow over the city. Her notebook was brimming with notes, her mind alive with possibilities. For the first time, she felt a sense of clarity—not just about the story she needed to write, but about the valley itself.

The Okanagan wasn't just a place of beauty and abundance. It was a place of resilience, a testament to the enduring spirit of those who had come before.

Chapter 31

The evening air in Kelowna was cool, carrying the faint scent of pine and the distant hum of traffic from Highway 97. Claire sat on the veranda of the B&B, her notebook open on her lap. The library visit had unearthed more than she had anticipated—stories of struggle and triumph, of families who had poured everything into the land only to see it slip away.

She stared at the title she'd written earlier, *'Preserving the Roots: The Fragile Legacy of the Okanagan's Vineyards.'* It felt right, but with it came a new wave of anxiety. Would Ethan trust her to tell the story in a way that honored his legacy? Could she balance truth with sensitivity?

Her phone buzzed, and she glanced at the screen. It was a text from Ethan.

"Are you free to talk? Need to clear the air."

Claire hesitated before typing back. *"Sure. Where?"*

A few moments later, his reply came through. *"Meet me at the lake. Same spot by the marina."*

The marina was quiet, the water reflecting the soft glow of the city lights. Claire spotted Ethan leaning against the railing, his hands tucked into his jacket pockets.

"Hey," she said as she approached, her voice tentative.

Ethan turned, offering a small smile. "Hey. Thanks for coming."

Claire leaned against the railing beside him, the silence between them stretching for a moment before he spoke.

"I've been thinking about what you said," Ethan began, his gaze fixed on the lake. "About the story."

"And?" Claire prompted, her voice steady despite the flutter of nerves in her chest.

"I want you to write it," he said finally, turning to meet her eyes. "But I need to know that it's not just about me or the vineyard. It has to be about something bigger—something that shows why this matters."

Claire nodded, relief washing over her. "That's exactly what I want to do. It's not just about you or this place—it's about the valley, the people, the history. I want to show the world why it's worth fighting for."

Ethan's expression softened, the tension in his shoulders easing. "Alright. But if at any point I feel like it's going too far, you have to promise me you'll pull back."

"Deal," Claire said without hesitation.

They stood in silence for a moment, the cool breeze brushing past them. Finally, Ethan broke the quiet with a wry smile. "You know, I didn't think I'd be trusting a writer to tell my story."

Claire laughed softly. "And I didn't think I'd be this invested in a vineyard."

Ethan's gaze lingered on her, something unspoken passing between them. "It's more than a vineyard," he said quietly.

"I know," Claire replied, her voice just as soft.

Back at the B&B later that night, Claire sat at her desk, the weight of Ethan's trust settling over her. She opened her laptop, the blank screen waiting for her to begin.

She took a deep breath and started to write:

The Okanagan Valley is more than a destination—it's a living story, told through its vines, its people, and its enduring spirit. It's a place where history meets the present, where legacies are born, and where the fight to preserve its soul is ongoing. This is the story of a land, a people, and the delicate balance they must maintain to survive.

Chapter 32

Claire sat in the local history section of the Okanagan Regional Library, her table piled high with books, maps, and old photographs. The library's quiet buzz faded as she immersed herself in the history of Kelowna—a narrative that felt as deeply rooted as the vineyards that now dominated the valley.

One book, *Early Days of the Okanagan,* painted a picture of a time before grapevines blanketed the hillsides. Claire learned that Kelowna's fertile soil had once been home to vast tobacco fields, cultivated by settlers in the late 19th and early 20th centuries. The industry thrived briefly, with leaves dried in wooden barns that dotted the landscape.

But tobacco farming gave way to fruit orchards as demand shifted. Claire flipped through pages filled with images of peach, apple, and cherry trees stretching as far as the eye could see. The early settlers had discovered that the Okanagan's warm climate and unique soil composition were perfect for growing stone fruits. By the 1930s, Kelowna had become synonymous with orchards, its fruit exported across the country.

Her pen scratched across her notebook as she jotted down notes. The transition from tobacco to fruit trees, and later to vineyards, mirrored the valley's evolution—a testament to the adaptability of its people and their deep connection to the land.

Another book drew her attention: *The Mission of Father Pandosy*. The leather-bound volume detailed the arrival of Father Charles Pandosy, a French Catholic priest who established a mission in the Okanagan in 1859. It was the first permanent European settlement in the region, and its influence rippled through the valley's development.

Claire lingered on an old photograph of the mission site, its wooden buildings simple yet sturdy. Father Pandosy had not only introduced Christianity to the area but also supported agricultural endeavors, helping settlers understand the land's potential.

As Claire turned the pages, she couldn't help but draw parallels between the valley's history and its present. Each chapter of Kelowna's past had been shaped by people who saw possibility where others saw wilderness—people like Ethan, who refused to let the land's story be rewritten by developers and corporations.

She made a note to visit the Father Pandosy Mission site. It was still preserved as a historical landmark, a place where she might gain a deeper understanding of the valley's origins.

Back at the B&B, Claire spread her notes across the bed, her thoughts whirring with ideas. The tobacco fields, the fruit orchards, the mission—they weren't just historical facts. They were threads that connected the valley's past to its present, revealing a tapestry of resilience and reinvention.

Opening her laptop, Claire began drafting a new section for her article:

Draft Excerpt:
Before the Okanagan Valley was known for its world-class vineyards, it was a patchwork of tobacco fields, fruit orchards, and missionary outposts. Each era brought with it a new wave of settlers and visionaries, drawn to the land's promise and potential.

The early tobacco farmers braved harsh winters and unpredictable markets, their dried leaves filling barns that dotted the landscape. As the valley's climate revealed itself to be better suited for fruit, the hillsides transformed into orchards that became the backbone of Kelowna's economy.

And before all of that, there was the Father Pandosy Mission—the first permanent European settlement in the valley. It was here that the seeds of agriculture were sown, where settlers learned to work with the land rather than against it.

These stories are the roots of the Okanagan, buried beneath the vineyards we see today. They remind us that the valley's beauty and abundance are not just gifts of nature, but the result of generations of effort and vision.

Claire sat back, rereading her words. The valley's story was coming into focus, and with it, her understanding of what lay beneath its surface.

But as she saved her draft, a familiar unease crept in. Marcy wouldn't see the value in this kind of story—not unless Claire could find a way to make it resonate on a deeper level.

Chapter 33

The unease lingered as Claire closed her laptop. She looked out the window of her B&B, the fading sunlight casting long shadows over the garden. The story she was uncovering felt more significant with each passing day, yet she couldn't shake the feeling that Marcy would want something more sensational.

Pushing the thought aside, Claire decided she needed to visit the Father Pandosy Mission the next morning. The site had played such a pivotal role in the valley's early history that it might provide the deeper resonance her story needed.

The next day dawned with the soft glow of a late autumn sun. Claire arrived at the Father Pandosy Mission, the grounds quiet except for the rustle of leaves in the breeze. The small cluster of buildings stood like sentinels of the past, their weathered wood exuding a sense of endurance.

She wandered through the mission's chapel, barns, and schoolhouse, each structure a glimpse into a simpler yet challenging way of life. Inside the chapel, light filtered through the narrow windows, illuminating the hand-carved pews and simple altar. Claire ran her fingers along the rough wood of the doorframe, imagining the settlers who had once gathered here.

A small plaque caught her eye, detailing Father Pandosy's vision for the area. It spoke of his belief in the land's potential, not just for agriculture but as a home for future generations. The words struck Claire:

"The land is a gift, not just for those who work it, but for those who will inherit its promise."

She jotted the quote into her notebook, her thoughts racing. It wasn't just about preserving the land—it was about passing something meaningful to the future. That was the heart of the Okanagan's story, and Ethan's struggle was a continuation of it.

As Claire returned to her car, her phone buzzed. It was a message from Marcy.

"We need to talk. Call me ASAP."

Claire hesitated, the weight of the text pressing down on her. She'd avoided confrontation for as long as she could, but the time had come to face it.

She found a quiet spot by Okanagan Lake, the water shimmering under the midday sun, and dialed Marcy's number.

"Claire," Marcy answered, her tone brisk. "Tell me you have something. The deadline's closing in, and I need to know what you're working with."

"I do," Claire said, steadying her voice. "But it's not the kind of story you're expecting. It's about the history of the valley, the people who've shaped it, and the fight to preserve its future."

Marcy sighed audibly. "History is great, Claire, but it doesn't sell magazines. I need drama. I need stakes."

"It has stakes," Claire insisted. "Ethan's vineyard is a microcosm of what's happening all over the valley. Developers are threatening to erase generations of work, and people are fighting to protect what matters to them. It's real, and it's compelling."

"Is Ethan willing to go on record?" Marcy asked.

Claire paused, choosing her words carefully. "He's cautious, but he's open to sharing his story if it's done right."

"Good," Marcy said, her tone softening slightly. "But you need more. A story like this needs to hit hard—it needs emotion, conflict, resolution. Find a way to make it resonate beyond the Okanagan."

"I'll do my best," Claire said, though doubt lingered in her chest.

After ending the call, she sat for a long time by the lake, watching the gentle ripples on the water. The conversation with Marcy had reignited her fears, but it also fueled her determination.

That evening, Claire revisited her draft, weaving in new insights from the Father Pandosy Mission. The article was evolving, its tone richer and more layered. She began to see it not just as a feature piece, but as a narrative that could inspire people to value what lay beneath the surface of their lives—whether it was a vineyard, a community, or their own history.

Chapter 34

Claire had heard the name Knox Mountain many times since arriving in Kelowna. The towering natural landmark stood as a sentinel over the city, its rugged beauty drawing hikers, cyclists, and dreamers alike. But she had never thought of it as more than a picturesque backdrop—until now.

It started with a conversation at the library. Claire had been flipping through an old book on Kelowna's development when an elderly woman at a nearby table struck up a conversation.

"That mountain has seen a lot," the woman said, her voice soft but certain. "It wasn't always the city park you see today."

Claire looked up, intrigued. "What do you mean?"

The woman smiled wistfully. "Before it became a park, Knox Mountain was privately owned. Families lived and worked on that land, tending livestock and planting crops. My grandfather used to tell me about a Czechoslovakia man who owned the mountain—a kind man who dreamed of making it a sanctuary for his family. But life has a way of testing us, doesn't it?"

Claire leaned in, her interest piqued. "What happened to him?"

The woman's expression darkened slightly. "He became ill. Back then, doctors weren't cheap, and hospitals were few and far between. He sold the mountain to pay his medical bills. Gave up everything he'd built so his family wouldn't lose him. But in the end, he passed away anyway, leaving his family with nothing but the memory of what they had."

The story hit Claire like a punch to the gut. "Do you know his name?"

"Joseph Frank Gregorvich," the woman admitted, her voice tinged with regret. "His story is buried beneath that mountain, in its soil and stones."

That afternoon, Claire drove to Knox Mountain Park, her thoughts heavy with the story. She parked at the base and started walking up one of the trails, the incline steep but manageable. The path wound through clusters of pine trees, their scent sharp and earthy in the crisp air.

As she reached a viewpoint, the city unfolded below her, Okanagan Lake shimmering in the sunlight. The mountain was quiet, save for the rustling of leaves and the occasional chirp of a bird. Claire sat on a large rock, her notebook open in her lap, and imagined what it must have been like to call this place home.

She jotted down notes as fragments of the story formed in her mind.

Draft Excerpt:

Knox Mountain stands as a symbol of Kelowna's endurance, its slopes a living history of the families who once called it their own. Among them was a man who dreamed of leaving a legacy, only to see it stripped away by the cruel hand of fate.

His story is not unique. The Okanagan Valley is filled with tales of sacrifice—of people who gave everything to hold onto what they loved, and sometimes lost it anyway.

But even in loss, their legacies endure. The mountain's trails, its trees, and the view it offers are all echoes of those who came before. Their sacrifices are what shaped this valley, giving it the resilience it needs to thrive.

As Claire closed her notebook, a strange sense of peace settled over her. The story of Knox Mountain wasn't just about loss—it was about what people were willing to do for those they loved.

She thought of Ethan, of his vineyard and the legacy he was fighting to preserve. The struggles of the past weren't so different from the struggles of the present. Beneath the surface, beneath the vineyards and mountains, the human story remained the same.

Chapter 35

Claire's day began in the Okanagan Regional Library once again, her curiosity about the valley's Indigenous history leading her to the cultural and historical archives. The Syilx Nation, also known as the Okanagan people, had left an indelible mark on the land long before settlers arrived. Their stories and traditions resonated deeply with the themes Claire had been uncovering in her research.

She was scrolling through a digital collection of historical photos and documents when a librarian approached her. "If you're interested in Syilx history, there's an elder, Thomas Cardinal, who gives talks at the Kelowna Heritage Museum. He's there today for a small presentation on the cultural significance of Okanagan Lake."

Excited by the possibility, Claire thanked the librarian and hurried to the museum.

The Kelowna Heritage Museum was a modest building, its exhibits filled with artifacts that told the story of the valley—from its earliest inhabitants to its modern-day transformation. Claire found herself in a cozy room at the back of the museum, where a small group had gathered to hear Thomas speak.

Thomas was a tall man with a commanding presence, his long hair streaked with silver and tied back neatly. His voice was calm but carried an authority that demanded attention as he began to speak.

"Our people, the Syilx, have lived in the Okanagan Valley for thousands of years," he said. "This land provided everything we needed—food, shelter, and a deep connection to the spirit of the world. Every lake, every mountain, every tree has meaning to us. They're not just resources, they're part of who we are."

He gestured toward a photograph of Okanagan Lake projected behind him. "You may have heard of N'ha-a-itk, what the settlers call Ogopogo. To my people, it's not a monster. It's a sacred being, a protector of the lake and the balance between land and water.

We honor it because it reminds us that we are stewards, not owners, of this place."

Claire's pen moved quickly across her notebook, capturing every word. The idea of N'ha-a-itk as a guardian rather than a monster struck her deeply. She had only known the myth as a tourist attraction, but hearing Thomas's explanation added layers of meaning she hadn't considered.

After the presentation, Claire approached Thomas, who greeted her warmly. "You have questions," he said, more a statement than a guess.

"I do," Claire admitted. "I'm a writer, and I've been researching the history of the Okanagan. The story of N'ha-a-itk and the Syilx people—it's so much richer than I realized. I want to share it, but I want to do it justice."

Thomas nodded. "The first step is understanding. Many people see this land as something to be conquered or used, but for us, it's alive. When you walk through the forests, do you feel the earth beneath your feet? Do you hear the water in the lake? That's where the real story lies—beneath the surface, in the roots and the spirit of the land."

Claire felt a chill at his words, not from the air but from their resonance. "It's beautiful," she said softly. "Thank you for sharing this with me."

Thomas gave her a small smile. "Share it with others, but do so with respect. These stories aren't just ours; they're the valley's, and the valley belongs to everyone who treats it with care."

That evening, back at the B&B, Claire began weaving what she had learned into her article.

Draft Excerpt:
Before the settlers planted the first vines, before the orchards blanketed the hills, the Okanagan Valley was home to the Syilx people. They understood the land not as a possession but as a partner, a sacred gift to be nurtured and respected.

The legend of N'ha-a-itk, the guardian of Okanagan Lake, is more than a tale—it's a lesson. It reminds us that the balance of nature is fragile and that our role is to protect it, not exploit it.

Today, the vineyards of the Okanagan echo that same balance. The soil, the water, and the air work together to create something beautiful, but only if they are treated with care. Beneath the vineyards lies not just the history of settlers, but the wisdom of the Syilx people, whose relationship with the land continues to guide us.

Claire saved her draft and leaned back in her chair, a quiet sense of purpose settling over her. This was the story she wanted to tell—not just about wine or tourism, but about the heart of the valley and the people who had shaped it.

Chapter 36

Claire's fingers hovered over the keyboard the next morning, reluctant to hit "send." The article wasn't finished, not really, but Marcy had been relentless. Claire finally pressed the button, sending her draft off with a sigh of trepidation. It wasn't long before her phone buzzed, Marcy's name flashing on the screen.

"Claire," Marcy began, her tone clipped. "I just read the draft. It's…interesting."

"Interesting?" Claire repeated, wary.

"You've clearly put a lot of thought into this," Marcy continued, "But I'm not sure it's what we're looking for. The history is compelling, and the Indigenous angle is nice, but it feels…niche. I need something that grabs readers, something with a hook."

Claire felt her chest tighten. "A hook? This is about more than just a catchy headline,

Marcy. It's about showing people the layers of this place, the sacrifices, the resilience—"

"I get that," Marcy interrupted. "But let's be honest. Most readers aren't going to care about a vineyard's struggle to stay afloat or the spiritual significance of a lake monster. They want drama. Conflict. You need to make it pop, Claire, or this isn't going to work."

"Pop?" Claire echoed, her frustration rising. "This isn't some fluff piece for a travel brochure. It's real, Marcy. These stories matter."

Marcy sighed, the sound laced with exasperation. "Look, I don't have time to argue. I need you to think about what will sell. Maybe dig deeper into the developers trying to buy out these vineyards. Or better yet, find some dirt on Ethan's operation. There's always a scandal hiding somewhere."

Claire's jaw dropped. "You want me to create conflict where there isn't any?"

"I want you to give readers a reason to care," Marcy snapped. "You're a journalist, Claire, not a historian. Find the tension, or find a new angle. You've got 48 hours."

The line went dead before Claire could respond, leaving her staring at her phone in disbelief.

For the rest of the day, Claire wrestled with her emotions. She knew Marcy had a point—journalism often thrived on drama—but the thought of twisting the truth made her stomach churn. Ethan's story, the valley's story, wasn't about manufactured conflict. It was about people fighting to preserve something they loved.

Late that afternoon, she decided to clear her head with a walk along the boardwalk. The air was crisp, the lake shimmering under the pale autumn sun. Families strolled by, children's laughter mingling with the distant hum of boats. But even the tranquility of the scene couldn't quiet her inner turmoil.

As she approached a quiet stretch of the boardwalk, she spotted Ethan sitting on a bench, his posture relaxed but his gaze fixed on the water. She hesitated, unsure if she wanted to share her frustrations, but he looked up and spotted her.

"Hey," he said, gesturing to the empty spot beside him. "You look like you're carrying the weight of the world."

Claire sank onto the bench with a sigh. "Marcy called."

Ethan raised an eyebrow. "Let me guess—she didn't love the article?"

"She wants more conflict," Claire admitted. "She said it's too niche, too…nice. She even suggested digging up dirt on your vineyard to make it more dramatic."

Ethan's expression darkened. "That's ridiculous. Is that what you're going to do?"

"Of course not," Claire said quickly. "But I don't know how to make her see the value in what I've written. It's frustrating."

Ethan leaned back, his gaze returning to the lake. "You have to decide who you're writing for, Claire. If it's for her, then you'll have to play her game. But if it's for the valley—for the people who've lived and worked here—then you stick to your truth."

Claire looked at him, his words resonating deeply. "You make it sound so simple."

"It's not," Ethan admitted. "But the best things never are."

That evening, Claire sat in her room, staring at her laptop. Marcy's deadline loomed, but for the first time, she felt certain about her next step. She began revising her draft, not to appease Marcy, but to make the story resonate with the people who knew the valley's heart.

Draft Revision Excerpt:
The Okanagan Valley isn't just a destination; it's a tapestry of stories woven into its hills and waters. Beneath the vineyards, beneath the lake's surface, lie generations of sacrifice,

resilience, and hope. These stories aren't loud or dramatic—they're quiet, persistent, and deeply human.

As she typed, a thought struck her. If Marcy couldn't see the value in this story, maybe it was time to find someone who could.

Chapter 37

The atmosphere in the vineyard felt heavier that afternoon, the golden light of the setting sun casting long shadows over the rows of vines. Claire could sense Ethan's tension even before she approached him near the barn. His phone was clutched tightly in his hand, his jaw set in a hard line.

"What's wrong?" Claire asked, her voice tentative.

Ethan glanced at her, his eyes dark with frustration. "Developers. They've been circling like vultures, but now it's worse. They've made offers to some of my neighbors, and I heard one of them accepted. If they get enough land, they'll turn this entire area into another resort."

Claire's stomach twisted. "Another resort? That would completely change the valley."

Ethan nodded. "It's not just my vineyard at risk anymore. They'll carve up the land, destroy what makes this place special, and leave behind something shiny and soulless."

The weight of his words sank into Claire's chest. She thought back to the stories she'd uncovered—the settlers, the Syilx people, the generations of families who had poured their lives into the valley. Everything they had built was now under threat.

That night, Claire sat in her room, her thoughts racing. She pulled up her article draft, but the words suddenly felt inadequate. This wasn't just a story anymore—it was a call to action. She needed to dig deeper, to uncover who was behind the development plans and expose their intentions.

The next morning, armed with her notebook and recorder, Claire headed to a town hall meeting she'd seen advertised in the local paper. The meeting was small, but the tension in the room was palpable. A representative from the development company was presenting polished renderings of luxury resorts, complete with golf courses and high-end spas.

"We believe this project will bring significant economic growth to the Okanagan

Valley," the representative said, his voice smooth. "It's a win-win for everyone involved."

Claire glanced around the room, noting the skeptical expressions on the faces of local vineyard owners and farmers. When the floor opened for questions, Ethan stood up.

"What about the people who live and work here?" he asked, his tone sharp. "Your resorts might bring tourists, but what happens to the land? To the vineyards that have been here for generations?"

The representative offered a rehearsed smile. "We're committed to preserving the natural beauty of the area while enhancing its accessibility and appeal."

Ethan shook his head, his frustration evident. "That's not preservation. That's exploitation."

After the meeting, Claire found Ethan leaning against his truck in the parking lot, his frustration still simmering.

"I think I know what I need to do," Claire said, her voice steady.

Ethan looked at her, his gaze searching. "And what's that?"

"I'm going to write the article—exactly the way it needs to be written. Not just about your vineyard, but about all of this," she said, gesturing to the land around them. "The history, the people, the stakes. If Marcy doesn't want it, I'll find someone who does."

Ethan's expression softened, a flicker of hope in his eyes. "You're putting a lot on the line for this."

Claire smiled faintly. "So are you."

Chapter 38

The tension from the town hall meeting lingered as Claire sat in her car, the morning sunlight filtering through the windshield. She opened her laptop, her fingers hovering over the keyboard. The developers had a name—Relcor Vista Developments—and now she had a target.

Her first stop was the local records office. The clerk, a woman in her forties with a no-nonsense demeanor, greeted her with a skeptical glance as she explained her request.

"You're looking for development permits?" the clerk asked, her fingers poised over her keyboard.

"Yes," Claire replied, her voice steady. "I'm specifically interested in permits filed by

Relcor Vista Developments over the past year."

The clerk tapped a few keys before gesturing for Claire to follow her. They walked to a wall of filing cabinets, where the clerk pulled a folder marked Development Proposals.

"Here you go," she said, handing it to Claire. "But don't expect anything too exciting. These developers are good at keeping their plans vague."

Claire spread the documents across a table, her eyes scanning each page. The permits were filled with technical jargon, but a few key details stood out. Relcor Vista Developments had acquired several parcels of land in the area, including one adjacent to Ethan's vineyard.

Her breath hitched as she noticed a proposal for a "luxury eco-resort" that would include a private golf course and a sprawling hotel complex. The wording emphasized sustainability and minimal environmental impact, but the scale of the project told a different story.

She snapped photos of the documents before heading to her next stop, the library's digital archives. If Relcor Vista was as polished as they seemed, they likely had a history of similar projects elsewhere.

Hours later, Claire's search bore fruit. Articles and reports from other regions painted a picture of a company skilled at selling grand visions but leaving communities with broken promises. In one case, a small town in the Rockies had been promised a "sustainable ski resort." The result? Half-finished construction sites and a local economy left in ruins.

She jotted down notes, her anger simmering. This wasn't just about Ethan's vineyard anymore, it was about the valley as a whole.

That evening, Claire met Ethan at the vineyard, her findings spread out on the table in the tasting room.

"Relcor Vista isn't what they claim to be," she said, pointing to the articles she had printed. "They've done this before—promise the world, then leave towns worse off than they found them."

Ethan leaned over the table, his brow furrowed as he read. "They're targeting more than just me," he said, his voice low. "If they get their way, this entire valley will change—and not for the better."

Claire nodded. "We need to stop them. And the first step is making people aware of what's at stake."

Ethan glanced at her, his expression a mix of gratitude and determination. "You're risking a lot for this."

"Maybe," Claire said softly.

The next morning, Claire began reaching out to vineyard owners, local farmers, and anyone else who might be affected by Relcor Vista's plans. Some were hesitant to speak, worried about backlash, but others shared their stories—of land they had already lost or feared losing, of a way of life they were desperate to protect.

Her article began to take shape, the words flowing with a sense of urgency and purpose.

Draft Excerpt:
The Okanagan Valley is at a crossroads. For generations, this land has been shaped by the hands of those who work it, its beauty preserved by people who see its worth beyond profit margins.

Now, it faces a new threat—a developer promising luxury at the expense of history, culture, and community. Beneath the vineyards lie stories of sacrifice, resilience, and hope. These are the stories we risk losing if we don't act.

As she finished typing, Claire leaned back in her chair, exhaustion mingling with a sense of accomplishment. The stakes had never been higher, but for the first time, she felt ready to face them.

Chapter 39

Claire spent the next few days arranging meetings with local vineyard owners and farmers, her notebook and recorder ready to capture their stories. Each visit took her deeper into the history of the Okanagan Valley, revealing tales of resilience, sacrifice, and an unyielding connection to the land.

Her first stop was the small, family-run Solara Vineyards. The granddaughter of the original owner, Anna Carmichael, greeted Claire warmly on the porch of their farmhouse. Her hair was streaked with silver, and her hands bore the marks of a lifetime spent working the vines.

"My grandfather started this place with nothing but a few borrowed tools and a dream," Anna said, leading Claire through the vineyard. The rows of vines stretched toward the horizon, their leaves rustling in the breeze.

Claire recorded as Anna continued. "Back then, this valley wasn't known for wine. It was orchards—peaches, apples, cherries. But my grandfather believed in the potential of these hills. He worked through harsh winters and blistering summers, sometimes barely scraping by. There were years when we thought we'd lose everything."

"What kept him going?" Claire asked.

Anna smiled faintly. "The land. He always said it had a soul, and it gave back what you put into it. Every harvest was a reminder of why he stayed."

At Hillside Orchards, Claire met with Jake Collins, whose family had been cultivating fruit trees since the 1920s. Jake was in his early sixties, his sun-weathered face breaking into a grin as he showed Claire the old barn where his grandfather had stored crates of apples bound for markets across Canada.

"Back in my granddad's day, they didn't have the technology we do now," Jake said. "Everything was done by hand. They'd pick fruit at dawn, load it into wagons, and haul it down to the packing house by horse."

Claire leaned against the barn door, imagining the scene. "It sounds grueling."

"It was," Jake said, his tone nostalgic. "But it was worth it. My grandfather always said the orchard wasn't just a business—it was a legacy. Something to pass down, something to be proud of."

In the southern part of the valley, Claire visited the historic Blackstone Ranch, now run by siblings who had turned part of their grandfather's land into a boutique vineyard. Lila Blackstone, the older of the two, poured Claire a glass of their Syrah as they sat on the patio overlooking the hills.

"Our grandfather used to grow hay and barley here," Lila said, gesturing to the fields. "He wasn't a winemaker, but he loved the land. During the Depression, he let neighbors graze their cattle here for free. Said it wasn't right to see families go hungry when he had the space to help."

Her brother, Marcus, nodded. "We like to think we're honoring that spirit by keeping the land productive. The vineyard is new, but it's rooted in the same values he taught us—community, hard work, and respect for the earth."

Each story Claire collected deepened her understanding of the valley and its people. The families she met weren't just working the land; they were preserving pieces of history, carrying forward the lessons of those who had come before them.

That evening, as Claire reviewed her notes, she felt a new sense of purpose. Relcor Vista Developments might see the valley as a blank canvas for profit, but she now understood it as a tapestry woven with the hopes, dreams, and sacrifices of generations.

Chapter 40

Claire sat at the desk in her B&B, her laptop open to a blank document. The stories she had collected over the past few days swirled in her mind, their voices echoing with resilience and pride. But as much as these tales inspired her, they also weighed heavily. The valley's history wasn't just a record of triumph—it was a testament to the struggles that had shaped it.

Her thoughts were interrupted by the chime of an incoming email. It was from Marcy.

Subject: Deadline Reminder
Claire,
I hope you're making progress. Remember, we need a strong angle for this piece—something that's going to hook readers and hold their attention. Don't forget about the

developers; there's drama there if you dig hard enough.

Looking forward to seeing what you've got.
-Marcy

Claire sighed, her frustration mounting. Marcy's single-minded pursuit of drama threatened to overshadow the heart of the valley's story. She couldn't let that happen. But Marcy's words had planted a seed. If she wanted to expose Relcor Vista Developments and the threat they posed, she needed to connect the dots and build a compelling case.

That afternoon, Claire drove to Ethan's vineyard. The air was crisp, and the vines glistened with the remnants of an early morning rain. She found Ethan in the barn, repairing a piece of equipment.

"You're getting good at showing up unannounced," Ethan said, glancing up with a faint smile.

Claire leaned against the doorframe. "And you're getting good at putting up with it."

Ethan chuckled, but his expression quickly turned serious as Claire explained her plan. "I want to include the developers in the article, but not in the way Marcy wants. I want to expose them for what they are—a threat to everything this valley stands for. But I need more than just stories. I need proof."

Ethan nodded slowly. "You're not wrong. But digging into people like that can get messy. Are you sure you're ready for it?"

"I don't have a choice," Claire said. "If I don't, who will?"

Ethan made a few calls, and by evening, they were seated in a dimly lit room at a local community center. A small group of vineyard owners and farmers had gathered, their faces reflecting a mix of determination and apprehension.

Claire introduced herself, explaining her intent to write an article that would shine a light on the developers' tactics and the stakes for the valley.

One man, his weathered hands gripping a cup of coffee, spoke first. "My family's owned our vineyard for three generations. Relcor Vista offered us a price that would've solved all our financial problems, but we said no. It's not just about money—it's about this land. It's who we are."

A woman in her forties added, "They're persistent. They've been targeting us for months, trying to convince us we can't make it on our own. It's like they're betting we'll give up."

Another voice chimed in. "They don't just want the land—they want control. Once they get a foothold, they'll turn this valley into something unrecognizable."

Claire listened intently, her pen flying across her notebook. Each story added another layer to the narrative she was building—a tapestry of resistance against a force that sought to erase the valley's soul.

As the meeting wrapped up, an elderly woman approached Claire. "You're brave to do this," she said, her voice low. "But be careful. Developers like this don't play fair. They'll go after you if they think you're a threat."

Claire swallowed hard, the weight of the warning settling over her. "Thank you. I'll be careful."

That night, back at her B&B, Claire opened her laptop and began typing.

Draft Excerpt:
The Okanagan Valley is not just a picturesque destination—it's a living history of perseverance and passion. For generations, its people have nurtured the land, creating a legacy that goes far beyond the wine in their glasses.

But this legacy is under threat. Relcor Vista Developments promises luxury and growth, but their track record tells a different story—a tale of broken promises and irreversible change.

The valley's people aren't giving up without a fight. They know what's at stake: their land, their identity, and their future. Beneath the vineyards lies not just the soil that sustains them, but the stories that define them.

As she finished the paragraph, a new thought struck Claire. This wasn't just a story anymore. It was a battle for the heart of the valley, and she was no longer an observer. She was part of it.

Chapter 41

The late afternoon sun bathed the backyard of the B&B in a golden glow as Claire sat on the veranda, sipping tea. She was flipping through her notes when the B&B owner, Margaret, appeared with a plate of cookies and a warm smile.

"You've been working hard," Margaret said, setting the plate on the small table beside Claire. "You should take a break."

Claire smiled, grateful for the gesture. "It's hard to stop when there's so much to uncover."

Margaret tilted her head thoughtfully. "Uncovering is good, but sometimes you need to feel the land, not just write about it. Come with me—I want to show you something."

Curious, Claire followed Margaret across the yard. They passed a small garden and a couple of fruit trees until they reached the far corner of the property. There, partially hidden by taller trees, stood a peculiar sight: a single, gnarled tree, its branches twisting and curling in unusual directions.

"It's beautiful," Claire said, stepping closer.

"It's unique," Margaret corrected, her voice soft but reverent. "This tree has been here for as long as I've owned the B&B, and likely for decades before that. Look at how it twists, almost like it's reaching in every direction at once."

Claire ran her fingers gently over the bark, its texture rough and uneven. "What caused it to grow like this?"

Margaret smiled mysteriously. "Some say it's the energy of the valley. Have you heard of Sedona, Arizona? How people go there for the energy vortexes?"

Claire nodded. "I've read about it. People say they feel more connected there, more alive."

"Well, I believe Kelowna has its own version of that," Margaret said, her voice dropping as if sharing a secret. "The Okanagan Valley has a special energy. You feel it in the way the lake sparkles, the way the vineyards thrive, and even in the long lives of the people who settle here. There's something about this place that keeps people young at heart."

Claire raised an eyebrow. "You think the energy here is why so many elderly people love Kelowna?"

Margaret chuckled. "Absolutely. You'll notice it if you look. People come here to retire, and they stay healthy for years longer than you'd expect. There's a vibrancy to this valley, something that makes you feel more connected to yourself, to the earth, and to the people around you. Even this tree—look at how it's thrived despite its odd shape. It's rooted in something bigger than itself."

Claire stood quietly, letting Margaret's words sink in. She thought back to her time in the valley—the serene mornings by the lake, the vibrant colors of the vineyards, and the stories she had collected. There was a rhythm to this place, an undercurrent of life that seemed to pulse through everything and everyone.

"It's fascinating," Claire said finally. "I've been so focused on the history and the people, but I hadn't considered the energy of the land itself."

Margaret patted her arm. "You're a writer, Claire. You feel things deeply—that's why you're here. Maybe this tree, this valley, has more to tell you than you realize."

That night, Claire sat at her desk, staring at her laptop. Margaret's words lingered in her mind, weaving themselves into the fabric of the story she was trying to tell.

Draft Excerpt:
The Okanagan Valley is more than its vineyards, its lake, or even its people. Beneath its surface lies an energy that defies explanation—a force that connects the past to the present, the land to those who call it home.

It's in the twisted branches of an old tree that has weathered decades of storms. It's in the laughter of retirees who seem ageless, drawn to the valley's embrace. And it's in the wine, each bottle holding the spirit of a place that is alive, vibrant, and unyielding.

This is the Okanagan. A place where history, energy, and resilience converge.

Claire leaned back in her chair, her chest swelling with a mix of inspiration and clarity. Margaret had given her more than just a story—she had given her a deeper understanding of the valley's essence.

Chapter 42

The next morning, Claire found Margaret in the kitchen, humming a tune as she prepared breakfast. The scent of freshly baked scones filled the air, mingling with the aroma of coffee.

"Morning," Claire greeted, pouring herself a cup of coffee.

"Morning," Margaret replied, her smile warm. "Did you sleep well after our little adventure in the backyard?"

Claire chuckled. "I did, though I couldn't stop thinking about what you said—about the energy of the valley."

Margaret set a plate of scones on the table and gestured for Claire to join her. "If you found that fascinating, I have another story for you. Have you heard of Mount Boucherie?"

Claire shook her head, intrigued.

"It's that big hill you see near West Kelowna," Margaret began, her voice taking on a storyteller's cadence. "But it's not just a hill—it's an ancient volcano. Millions of years ago, it erupted, shaping much of this valley. What you see now is just the remnant of its volcanic core. The rest has been eroded over time."

Claire leaned forward, captivated. "A volcano? I had no idea."

Margaret nodded. "It's true. That volcano is one of the reasons the soil in this valley is so rich. Volcanic soil is full of minerals that plants love, and it's one of the things that makes the Okanagan such a perfect place for growing grapes."

Claire took a sip of her coffee, her mind already spinning with connections. "So the valley's success as a wine region is partly thanks to an ancient eruption?"

"Exactly," Margaret said. "But it's more than just the soil. Volcanic regions have an energy of their own—powerful, transformative. Some people believe that energy still lingers here, infusing the land and everything that grows on it."

Claire stared out the window, her gaze drifting toward the hills in the distance. "It's incredible to think that something so destructive could leave behind something so beautiful."

Margaret smiled. "That's nature for you. It has a way of renewing itself, of turning chaos into creation. And that's part of what makes this valley so special. It's not just a place to live—it's a place to feel alive."

Later that day, Claire couldn't resist driving out to Mount Boucherie to see it for herself. The dormant volcano rose against the sky, its rugged slopes a reminder of the valley's tumultuous past.

Parking her car at a nearby trailhead, Claire hiked to a vantage point that offered a sweeping view of the Okanagan Valley. The vineyards stretched out like a patchwork quilt, their rows gleaming in the sunlight. Okanagan Lake sparkled in the distance, its waters cradling the hills that surrounded it.

She sat on a rock, her notebook in hand, and began to write.

Draft Excerpt:

Mount Boucherie stands as a silent witness to the Okanagan Valley's transformation. Once a volcano that spewed fire and ash, it now nurtures the very soil that feeds the valley's vineyards.

The volcanic energy of this land is more than a geological curiosity—it's a metaphor for the resilience and renewal that define this place. From the ancient Syilx stewards to the settlers who planted the first orchards, the valley has always been a testament to the power of creation and reinvention.

The Okanagan isn't just a destination; it's a living story, written in the layers of its soil, the rhythm of its seasons, and the enduring spirit of its people.

Curious and with a bit of time to spare, Claire decided to make a quick stop at **Volcanic Hills Estate Winery**, just minutes from where she had been reflecting on Mount Boucherie. The drive was short but scenic, the rolling vineyards illuminated by the afternoon sun.

The winery's modern design stood in striking contrast to the ancient land surrounding it. Inside, Claire was greeted by the rich aroma of oak barrels and the inviting warmth of the staff. She opted for a tasting, intrigued by their signature Volcanic Hills Gewürztraminer. As she sipped, the wine's bright floral notes and crisp finish felt like a direct expression of the land itself—complex, vibrant, and steeped in history.

From the patio, the view stretched across the valley, the rows of vines glinting in the golden light. With her notebook open beside her, Claire jotted down thoughts about the connection between the volcanic soil and the depth of flavor in the wine. It was another layer to the valley's story, one that reinforced the bond between the land and its people.

Chapter 43

Claire had spent the morning editing her latest draft, her thoughts still lingering on the B&B owner Margaret's words about the valley's energy. After lunch, Margaret appeared again, carrying two cups of tea and a mischievous glint in her eye.

"I see that look," Claire said with a smile. "You've got another story for me."

Margaret set the cups down and pulled out a folded map. "You could say that. Have you ever heard of ley lines?"

Claire frowned slightly. "I've read about them—lines of energy that some believe connect sacred sites around the world, right?"

Margaret nodded enthusiastically. "Exactly. And there's a theory that Kelowna sits at the intersection of some of these lines. It's another reason why this place feels so alive, so healing. You've felt it, haven't you?"

Claire hesitated, her mind flashing back to the sense of calm she'd felt under the twisted tree in Margaret's yard, the serenity of the lake, and the way the vineyards seemed to pulse with life. "Maybe," she admitted.

Margaret leaned in closer. "There's a legend among some of the locals, especially those who are sensitive to these things. They say the Syilx people knew about the energy here long before anyone else and considered the valley a place of spiritual power. It's why the land has always thrived, even when settlers faced impossible odds."

Intrigued, Claire decided to explore further. Margaret suggested she visit a woman named Irene, a local healer and energy worker who had lived in the valley her entire life.

That afternoon, Claire drove to Irene's home, a modest cottage nestled at the edge of a forested hill. Irene greeted her warmly, her silver hair braided and her voice rich with wisdom.

"You're here about the energy," Irene said without preamble, leading Claire to a sun-dappled garden.

Claire nodded, pulling out her notebook. "I've been hearing about it from different people. Margaret mentioned ley lines."

Irene smiled knowingly. "Margaret has a good intuition. The energy here isn't just about ley lines, though—it's about the land itself. The lake, the hills, the volcanic soil— they all work together, like a symphony. People come here for the wine, the views, the lifestyle, but what they don't realize is they're also coming to heal."

Claire tilted her head. "Heal how?"

Irene gestured toward the garden. "Emotionally. Spiritually. Sometimes even physically. There's a reason so many retirees settle here, and it's not just the weather. This place has a way of soothing the soul. The Syilx people understood that. They believed the lake and its surroundings were gifts from the Creator, places where people could find balance."

As Irene spoke, Claire felt a tingling awareness that she'd been experiencing this energy all along. It was in the way the vineyards seemed to hum with life, in the calm she felt walking by the lake, in the renewed purpose she'd found since arriving in the valley.

"It's funny," Claire said. "I came here to write a story about vineyards and wine, but the more I learn, the more I realize this valley is about so much more than that."

Irene smiled gently. "The land gives more than it takes. But it's up to us to honor that balance."

That evening, Claire sat on the veranda of the B&B, her laptop open as she began typing a new section of her article.

Draft Excerpt:
The Okanagan Valley isn't just a feast for the senses; it's a balm for the soul. Beneath its vineyards and sparkling lake lies an energy that has drawn people here for centuries.

The Syilx people understood this, seeing the land as a place of healing and balance. Today, visitors come for the wine and the views, but they often leave with something they didn't expect—renewed spirits, lighter hearts, a sense of wholeness.

This valley isn't just a destination; it's a sanctuary.

As the stars emerged overhead, Claire closed her laptop, a sense of calm washing over her. The valley's energy had worked its magic on her, too, and she knew her story was beginning to reflect that truth.

Chapter 44

Ethan's text arrived, interrupting Claire's focused effort to organize her notes.

Ethan:

Feel like a change of pace? Be ready for dancing. I'll pick you up at 9.

Claire raised an eyebrow at the message, her curiosity piqued. She replied with a quick thumbs-up emoji and hurried to get ready, wondering what he had planned.

When Ethan arrived, he was leaning casually against his truck, looking rugged in a plaid button-up shirt, jeans, and worn cowboy boots. Claire stepped out onto the porch, her curiosity evident.

"So, are you going to tell me where we're going?" she asked.

Ethan grinned. "Nope. But trust me—you'll like it."

Claire laughed as they pulled into the parking lot of the OK Corral Cabaret. The neon-lit sign glowed against the darkening sky, and the sound of country music spilled out into the crisp night air.

"Line dancing?" she asked, a note of amusement in her voice.

Ethan chuckled. "Not just line dancing. This place is a Kelowna institution. If you're going to write about the valley, you need to see all of it—including this side."

They stepped inside, and Claire was immediately struck by the lively atmosphere. The wooden floors gleamed under the glow of string lights, and the dance floor was filled with couples swaying to the music. A sense of nostalgia hung in the air, mingling with the scent of beer and barbecue.

"This place has been around forever," Ethan said as they found a table near the edge of the dance floor. "A lot of locals have celebrated birthdays, anniversaries, and even a few breakups right here."

Claire scanned the room, her gaze landing on the center of the dance floor. "Please tell me that's not where the mechanical bull comes out."

Ethan grinned. "Oh, it is. But only on Thursday nights. They clear the floor, and the bull rises right out of the middle like it's the star of the show. It's kind of a tradition around here."

Claire raised an eyebrow, her curiosity piqued. "Have you ridden it?"

Ethan laughed, shaking his head. "Not a chance. But my sister did. She was here for her bachelorette party, and her friends dared her to get on. She made it a whole eight seconds before she went flying. Said it was the highlight of the night—until she woke up the next morning and couldn't move."

Claire laughed, imagining the scene. "Sounds like a brave woman. As for me, I think I'll pass. I'd rather not become the next Thursday night spectacle."

"Suit yourself," Ethan teased. "But watching the rookies try? That's half the fun."

They ordered beers, and Ethan leaned back in his chair, watching the dancers move to the upbeat rhythm of the music. "I've been coming here for years," he said. "It's the kind of place where everyone lets loose a little. You can't take yourself too seriously when you're trying to line dance."

Claire took a sip of her beer, relaxing into the easy atmosphere. "So, are you going to make me line dance?"

"Oh, definitely," Ethan said, his grin widening. "But first, let's enjoy the show."

When a slower song began to play, Ethan stood and offered his hand. "Come on. Let's see if we can avoid stepping on each other's toes."

Claire hesitated but took his hand, allowing him to lead her to the dance floor. As they began to sway, she felt a surprising ease settle over her. Ethan's hand rested lightly on her waist, guiding her with a confidence that belied his earlier teasing about his dancing skills.

"You're better at this than you let on," Claire said, looking up at him.

Ethan smirked. "Don't spread that around. I've got a reputation to protect."

The music picked up again, and Ethan pulled Claire into a line-dancing lesson. She stumbled over her feet, laughing so hard at her own missteps that she could barely keep up.

"You're doing great," Ethan teased, his voice warm.

"I'm a disaster," Claire shot back, grinning. "But at least I'm consistent."

As they left the cabaret, the cool night air wrapped around them, carrying the faint sounds of laughter and music from inside. They walked slowly toward Ethan's truck, the energy of the night lingering between them.

"Thanks for tonight," Claire said softly, glancing at him. "I didn't realize how much I needed this."

Ethan stopped and turned to her, his expression warm but searching. "You've been so focused on everything—your article, this valley, even everyone else's stories. I just wanted to give you a moment to breathe. To just… be."

Claire smiled, the sincerity in his voice striking a chord deep within her. "Well, mission accomplished. Tonight was perfect."

They stood there for a moment, the cool air amplifying the heat that seemed to radiate between them. Ethan reached up and tucked a loose strand of hair behind her ear, his touch lingering just a moment longer than necessary.

"Claire," he murmured, his voice barely above a whisper.

She looked up at him, her heart pounding. The space between them seemed to dissolve as he leaned in, giving her just enough time to stop him if she wanted to. But she didn't.

His lips met hers, gentle at first, then deepening as the moment stretched. It was a kiss filled with unspoken emotions, with gratitude, with a connection that neither of them had expected but could no longer ignore.

When they finally pulled apart, Claire felt breathless, her cheeks warm despite the cool night. Ethan's hand rested lightly on her arm, his eyes searching hers.

"I've been wanting to do that for a while," he admitted, a sheepish grin tugging at his lips.

Claire laughed softly, her voice tinged with nervous excitement. "I'm glad you did."

They stood there for another moment, the night suddenly feeling much quieter, much more intimate. Without another word, Ethan opened the truck door for her, and Claire climbed in, her heart still racing.

As they drove back, the silence between them was comfortable, filled with the kind of understanding that only came from sharing something real. For the first time in a long time, Claire felt like she was exactly where she was meant to be.

Chapter 45

Claire sat at her desk in the B&B, a sea of papers, articles, and maps spread out before her. The room was quiet except for the rhythmic tapping of her pen against the notebook. Relcor Vista Developments had been a shadowy presence in her research—a company with a growing portfolio of properties, but very little public scrutiny.

Deciding she needed firsthand accounts, Claire arranged to meet several locals who had mentioned conflicts with the company.

Her first stop was a small orchard at the edge of town. The owner, an elderly man named Tom, greeted her with a firm handshake and a wary look.

"They came a few years back," Tom began, leading Claire to a bench under a sprawling apple tree. "Said they wanted to buy my land for some new luxury homes. Told me it'd be worth a fortune, more than I could make selling fruit in ten years."

Claire leaned forward. "And did you consider it?"

Tom nodded, his gaze drifting to the orchard. "At first. My kids didn't want to take over the farm, and the money sounded good. But when I started asking questions—about what they'd do with the land, about environmental protections—they got cagey. Tried to pressure me, said I'd regret not selling."

"And did you?" Claire asked softly.

Tom's lips tightened into a thin line. "No. But I've seen what happens to people who don't sell. They find ways to make life harder—buy up land around you, cut off access to water. My neighbor had to move because of it."

Claire's next interview was with a young couple, Lisa and Jordan, who had inherited a small vineyard from Jordan's grandparents.

"We held out as long as we could," Lisa said, her voice trembling. "They bought the land next to us and started construction. Trucks, noise, dust—it made running the vineyard impossible. They knew what they were doing."

Jordan nodded grimly. "When we finally sold, they didn't even give us a fair price. They knew we didn't have a choice."

As the day wore on, Claire pieced together a troubling pattern. Relcor Vista wasn't just a development company—they were a machine, systematically acquiring land and pressuring those who resisted. The valley's charm, its balance between progress and preservation, was being threatened by their relentless expansion.

Claire returned to her room that evening, her mind racing. She opened her laptop and began drafting her notes:

Draft Excerpt:
The Okanagan Valley is more than its picturesque vineyards and shimmering lake—it's a community. A fragile balance between tradition and growth. But that balance is under threat.

Relcor Vista Developments markets itself as a partner in progress, but the stories of those who've encountered them tell a different tale. Farmers, vineyard owners, and families with roots in this valley have faced pressure, manipulation, and loss, their land becoming the foundation for luxury developments that cater to outsiders.

Beneath the vineyards lies a struggle—a fight to protect not just the land, but the heart of the valley.

Claire leaned back in her chair, her chest tight with the weight of the stories she'd heard. This wasn't just a feature article anymore. It was a responsibility.

But as she stared at her notes, doubt began to creep in. Exposing Relcor Vista would mean confronting powerful forces. And what if Ethan wasn't ready for the fallout her article could bring?

Her phone buzzed, pulling her out of her thoughts. It was a text from Ethan.

Ethan:

How's the article coming?

Claire hesitated, then typed a reply.

Claire:

It's turning into something bigger than I expected. Can I come by tomorrow?

Ethan:

Always.

Chapter 46

The morning air was crisp as Claire pulled into Ethan's vineyard, her car tires crunching softly over the gravel. Ethan was waiting near the barn, leaning casually against the doorframe, his sleeves rolled up and his hands already marked with the dirt of the day's work. He straightened when he saw her, his easy smile tempered by a quiet curiosity.

"Right on time," he said, his tone light but his eyes searching hers. "Coffee's still warm if you want a cup."

Claire returned his smile but shook her head. "Thanks, but I think we need to talk first."

Ethan's expression shifted, his brow furrowing as he stepped aside, gesturing toward a shaded bench near the trellis. "Alright. Let's sit."

They walked in silence, the vineyard around them buzzing softly with life. The bench overlooked a row of vines heavy with ripening fruit dedicated for ice wine, the lake shimmering faintly in the distance. Claire settled beside him, her notebook already in her hands.

"I've been digging into Relcor Vista," she began, her voice steady but low. "What I've found…it's worse than I thought."

Ethan leaned forward, resting his elbows on his knees. "Go on."

Claire opened the notebook, flipping to the pages she'd marked with interviews and notes. "They're not just buying land. They're pressuring people—families, farmers, small vineyard owners. If someone doesn't sell, they make life unbearable. I've spoken to people who've had their water access cut off, who've lost business because of their construction, who've been forced out."

Ethan's jaw tightened as he scanned the pages, his hands curling into fists. "I knew they were aggressive, but this… Claire, this is a whole other level."

"It's systematic," she continued. "And it's erasing the history of this valley. The people, the stories, the heart of it all—it's being buried under their developments."

Ethan closed the notebook gently and turned to her. "And you're going to write about this? Expose them?"

Claire nodded. "I have to. But I'm not just writing an exposé. I want people to understand what's at stake—why this valley matters, why it's worth protecting."

Ethan was quiet for a moment, his gaze fixed on the horizon. "You're putting yourself in the line of fire, you know that."

Claire met his eyes, her voice firm. "I know. But it's the right thing to do."

Ethan exhaled deeply, running a hand through his hair. "Then you'll have my support. Whatever you need."

They spent the next hour walking the vineyard. Ethan spoke about his family's history on the land, how his grandparents had planted the first vines, how every decision he made was about honoring their legacy. He shared his fears—about what would happen if developers like Relcor Vista gained more ground, about how easy it was to lose sight of what truly mattered.

As they reached the edge of the property, Claire paused, her gaze sweeping over the vines. "Do you ever think about what's beneath all of this?" she asked. "The history, the lives, the stories that shaped this place?"

Ethan smiled faintly. "All the time. It's why I do this. The land isn't just dirt and roots—it's memories. It's sacrifices and dreams. Keeping that alive—that's the real work."

Claire nodded, her heart swelling with a quiet resolve. "That's what I want to capture in the article. What lies beneath the vineyards. The roots of this place."

Ethan turned to her, his expression softening. "Then you're the right person to tell it."

As Claire drove back to the B&B, Ethan's words lingered in her mind. Beneath the vineyards wasn't just a metaphor anymore—it was the essence of her story. The valley's beauty wasn't just in its views or its wine; it was in the people who had fought to preserve its soul.

She knew the article wouldn't be easy to write, and even harder to publish. But for the first time in her career, Claire felt like she was writing something that truly mattered.

Chapter 47

Claire sat at the B&B's kitchen table, the comforting aroma of freshly baked bread filling the air. Margaret bustled about, humming softly as she poured steaming cups of tea. The morning light filtered through the lace curtains, casting intricate patterns across the wooden surfaces.

"I thought you could use a little something to go with all that thinking," Margaret said, setting a plate of warm buns in front of Claire.

Claire smiled, grateful for the gesture. "You read my mind. I've been buried in research lately, but it's still not enough. I feel like there's something I'm missing—something deeper."

Margaret took a seat across from her, her expression thoughtful. "Have you looked into the Indigenous history of the valley? The Syilx people have been here far longer than any vineyard or orchard. Their connection to the land runs deep."

Claire leaned forward, her notebook at the ready. "I've touched on it briefly, but I'd love to know more. Do you know much about their history?"

Margaret nodded. "The Syilx people are the original stewards of this valley. For thousands of years, they've lived in harmony with the land, understanding its rhythms and respecting its sacred spaces. One of the most significant areas is the lake itself. They believe it's a source of life, a spiritual connection to their Creator."

Margaret paused, her gaze distant. "There's a story my grandmother used to tell about a sacred grove near Okanagan Lake. The Syilx would gather there for ceremonies, honoring the land and seeking guidance. When settlers arrived, many of these sacred spaces were disrupted, but the memories remain in the hearts of those who know."

Claire jotted down notes, the weight of the valley's layered history settling over her. "It's heartbreaking to think about how much has been lost."

Margaret sighed. "It is. But it's also why the Syilx people fight so hard to preserve what's left. They see the land as more than just a resource—it's a part of their identity, their soul."

As they sipped their tea, Margaret shared another story. "There's a legend about a Syilx elder who once spoke to a gathering of settlers and Indigenous people. He said the land would always give back to those who treated it with respect, but it would withhold its blessings from those who didn't. It's a lesson that's as relevant now as it was then."

Claire felt a shiver run through her, the truth of the elder's words resonating deeply. "Do you think there are still places like that sacred grove?"

Margaret smiled softly. "Oh, I'm sure of it. The energy of this valley is undeniable. You felt it under the tree in my backyard, didn't you? That's just one small example. There are places here where you can almost hear the land speaking—if you're willing to listen."

As the conversation wound down, Claire closed her notebook, her mind buzzing with new insights. The Syilx connection to the land wasn't just history—it was a living, breathing part of the valley's identity.

"I think I need to include this in my article," Claire said. "It's such an important part of the story."

Margaret nodded. "Good. The valley isn't just about vineyards and development. It's about the people who have cared for it, who have poured their hearts into it. Don't forget their voices, Claire."

Claire stood, a renewed sense of purpose guiding her steps. "Thank you, Margaret. This means more to me than you know."

As she returned to her room, Claire began drafting a new section of her article, weaving in the stories Margaret had shared. Beneath the vineyards, she thought again. The phrase wasn't just about the soil—it was about everything that had come before, everything that made the valley what it was.

Chapter 48

Claire was at Ethan's vineyard when the neighbor, breathless and hurried, pulled up in a dusty truck. "There's a group gathering near Lakeview Ridge. Relcor Vista's breaking ground—right on a piece of old orchard land. People are trying to stop them."

Ethan's expression darkened, his jaw tightening as he grabbed his jacket. "Let's go," he said to Claire without hesitation.

She followed him to his truck, her heart racing. This wasn't just another story—this was happening now, and it was personal.

As they approached the site, the scene came into view. A dozen locals stood in a loose line, their faces a mix of anger and determination. Bulldozers idled in the background, their sheer presence an ominous threat to the land. A representative from Relcor Vista, clad in a suit that seemed absurdly out of place, stood with arms crossed, flanked by a pair of security guards.

Claire stepped out of the truck, her notebook in hand, as Ethan strode purposefully toward the group.

"Ethan, glad you're here," said Tom, the orchard owner Claire had interviewed earlier. He gestured toward the machines. "They're trying to push through the old laws about preserving agricultural land. If they win here, it sets a precedent for the whole valley."

Ethan nodded grimly, his eyes scanning the group. "We can't let that happen."

Claire moved to the edge of the gathering, her pen flying across the page as she captured every detail—the desperation in the locals' voices, the tension in the air, the way the land itself seemed to stand as a silent witness.

A woman raised her voice. "This orchard was planted by my grandfather. He built this place from nothing, and now they want to turn it into condos? Over my dead body."

Another man chimed in. "They don't care about the valley—they care about money. If we let them start here, what's stopping them from taking more?"

The Relcor Vista representative stepped forward, his tone clipped and condescending.

"We have all the proper permits. You're trespassing, and we'll call the authorities if you don't disperse."

The crowd didn't budge.

Ethan stepped forward, his voice calm but firm. "You might have your permits, but this isn't just about paperwork. It's about respecting the people who've lived here, who've worked this land for generations. You can't bulldoze that away."

The man sneered. "Respect doesn't pay the bills. Progress does."

Claire felt a surge of frustration, her pen trembling in her hand. This was exactly what she had been uncovering—the arrogance, the disregard for the valley's history and people. She stepped forward, surprising even herself.

"If you think this is progress," she said, her voice steady, "You're not looking at the bigger picture. The valley isn't just land to develop— it's a community, a legacy. You're erasing something that can't be replaced."

The man scoffed, but Claire didn't back down. She felt Ethan's steady presence beside her, a silent show of support.

As the tension reached its peak, the sound of sirens broke through the air. A police car pulled up, its lights flashing. The officer stepped out, his expression neutral but firm.

"Alright, folks," he said. "Let's keep this peaceful. What's going on here?"

Tom stepped forward. "We're trying to stop them from breaking ground on this land. It's part of our valley's history."

The officer nodded slowly, his gaze moving between the locals and the Relcor Vista team. "Let's all step back for now. Everyone deserves to be heard."

The group dispersed slightly, but the energy remained charged. Ethan turned to Claire, his expression heavy. "This fight isn't over," he said quietly. "But it's going to take more than a few voices to stop them."

Claire nodded, her mind already spinning. "That's why I'm writing this. People need to see what's at stake, to understand what's beneath the vineyards, what they're really fighting for."

Ethan's gaze softened as he looked at her. "You've got a way of making people listen, Claire. Don't stop now."

That night, back at the B&B, Claire sat at her laptop, her fingers flying over the keys. The protest was a turning point—not just for the valley, but for her story. She began weaving the personal accounts she'd gathered, the raw emotion of the day, and the undeniable truth of what was happening.

Draft Excerpt:
The Okanagan Valley isn't just a collection of picturesque vineyards and tourist attractions. It's a living, breathing community, rooted in stories of resilience and tradition. But those roots are being threatened by the relentless march of development, led by corporations like Relcor Vista.

The fight isn't just about land; it's about identity. It's about honoring the people who have poured their lives into this place, whose sacrifices and dreams are woven into the fabric of the valley.

As she saved her work, Claire felt the weight of the day settle over her. The fight was far from over, but for the first time, she felt like she was doing something that truly mattered.

Chapter 49

The sun hung low in the sky as Claire arrived at Ethan's vineyard. The golden light bathed the rows of vines, casting long shadows across the land. Ethan was waiting for her near the barn, leaning against his truck with a contemplative look on his face.

"You look serious," Claire said as she approached, her notebook tucked under her arm.

Ethan straightened, offering a faint smile. "There's something I want to show you."

Claire raised an eyebrow. "Another one of your secrets?"

Ethan chuckled softly but didn't answer. Instead, he gestured for her to follow him.

They walked through the vineyard, the hum of insects and the occasional rustle of leaves the only sounds. Ethan led her to a secluded section at the edge of the property, where the vines grew in irregular patterns, their roots twisting through the rocky soil.

"This is where it all started," he said, his voice quiet.

Claire looked around, noting the wild, untamed feel of the area. "What do you mean?"

Ethan crouched down, running his fingers over the gnarled base of one of the vines. "These are the original vines my grandparents planted when they first bought this land. They were told it wouldn't work—that the soil was too rocky, the climate too harsh. But they didn't listen."

Claire knelt beside him, her fingers brushing against the rough bark of the vine. "They proved everyone wrong."

Ethan nodded, his gaze distant. "It wasn't easy. There were years when they barely broke even, when droughts or late frosts nearly wiped out the crops. But they held on. This vineyard wasn't just a business to them—it was their legacy, their connection to the land."

Ethan stood and motioned for Claire to follow him again. They climbed a small hill that overlooked the vineyard, the lake shimmering in the distance. At the top, Ethan pointed to a small, weathered bench beneath a sprawling oak tree.

"My grandfather built that bench," he said. "He used to sit there after a long day and talk about the land—how it had a soul, how it remembered everyone who worked it. He said if you listened closely, you could hear the stories beneath the soil."

Claire's chest tightened as she took in the scene. The vineyard wasn't just rows of vines or a plot of land—it was a living testament to resilience, love, and sacrifice.

As they sat on the bench, Ethan leaned back, his expression contemplative. "A few years ago, Relcor Vista approached me. Offered me more money than I'd ever dreamed of to sell this place. It was tempting—especially when I thought about how much easier life would be without the constant fight to keep this going."

"But you said no," Claire said softly.

"I said no," Ethan confirmed. "Because this place isn't just mine. It's my family's story. It's their dreams, their struggles, their triumphs. If I sold it, it'd be like erasing all of that. And I couldn't do it."

Claire felt a lump form in her throat. "That's what I want people to understand when they read my article. This valley—it's not just about the wine or the views. It's about the people who've poured their hearts into it."

Ethan turned to her, his gaze steady. "Then tell them. Tell them everything. And don't hold back."

As the sun dipped below the horizon, painting the sky in hues of orange and pink, Claire felt a deep sense of clarity. Beneath the vineyards lay more than just roots. There were stories of hope, resilience, and connection—stories she was determined to bring to light.

"Thank you for sharing this with me," she said, her voice barely above a whisper.

Ethan smiled, a soft warmth in his eyes. "Thank you for listening."

Chapter 50

Claire sat at the small desk in her B&B room, surrounded by a chaos of notes, books, and photos. The stories she'd gathered over the past weeks were more than just research—they were pieces of a puzzle, and now it was time to assemble them into something meaningful.

The cursor blinked on her laptop screen as she stared at the blank document. Taking a deep breath, she began to type:

Draft Excerpt:
The Okanagan Valley is a place of beauty and abundance, its rolling vineyards and shimmering lake drawing visitors from around the world. But beneath the surface lies a deeper story—one of resilience, sacrifice, and

a community's unyielding connection to the land.

This valley wasn't always covered in vines. It began with the Syilx people, who lived in harmony with its rhythms, treating the land as a sacred trust. Later came settlers, braving harsh winters and uncertain markets to farm tobacco and fruit. Each generation added its own chapter to the valley's story, adapting to the land while preserving its spirit.

Today, that story is at a crossroads. Developers like Relcor Vista are rewriting the landscape, threatening to erase the history embedded in its soil. But the people of the valley—the farmers, winemakers, and families who have fought to preserve this place—are determined not to let that happen.

Beneath the vineyards lies more than just roots. There are stories of love and loss, of dreams realized and dreams deferred. These stories remind us that the valley's beauty is not just a gift of nature, but a testament to the people who have poured their hearts into it.

Claire paused, rereading the words. They felt raw and honest, but there was still more to say. She pulled out her notebook, flipping to the pages filled with Ethan's story—the sacrifices his family had made, the decision to hold onto the vineyard despite overwhelming pressure to sell.

She began typing again, weaving his experiences into the narrative:

Draft Excerpt:
Ethan's vineyard is more than a business; it's a living legacy. His grandparents planted the first vines, defying skeptics who said the rocky soil wouldn't support grapes. They nurtured those vines through droughts, frosts, and lean years, believing in the land's potential.

When developers came calling, offering a fortune for the property, Ethan said no. For him, selling the land would have been like erasing his family's history. "This place isn't just mine," he told me. "It's my family's story. It's their dreams, their struggles, their triumphs."

As the article took shape, Claire felt the weight of the valley's history settling over her. Each story she included added depth, from the Syilx elder's wisdom about respecting the land to Margaret's tales of the valley's healing energy.

She wanted readers to see the valley as she had come to see it—not just as a picturesque destination, but as a place with a soul.

By the time she finished, the room was dark, the only light coming from her laptop screen. Claire leaned back in her chair, exhausted but satisfied. She'd written something true, something that mattered.

But as she saved the draft, a pang of doubt crept in. Would Marcy see the value in this? Would readers care about the stories of a small valley in British Columbia?

Claire pushed the thoughts aside. For now, the story was hers, and she'd told it the best way she knew how.

Chapter 51

The morning mist clung to the vineyard as Claire parked her car and made her way to Ethan's barn. The scent of freshly turned soil mingled with the sweetness of ripened grapes. She had shared her draft with him the previous evening, and now, as she approached, her stomach twisted with anticipation.

Ethan was by the barn, loading tools into the back of his truck. His posture was tense, his movements precise and deliberate. Claire hesitated before calling out.

"Morning," she said, trying to keep her voice light.

Ethan glanced over his shoulder, his expression unreadable. "Morning."

Claire stepped closer, the weight of his silence pressing down on her. "Did you read it?"

He nodded, setting down a spade with more force than necessary. "I did."

"And?" Claire prompted, her voice catching slightly.

Ethan turned to face her fully, his brow furrowed. "You're a hell of a writer, Claire. But some of what you included—it's personal. About my family, my choices. I wasn't expecting you to lay it all bare like that."

Claire's heart sank. "I thought it was important. Your story—it's part of what makes the valley so special. People need to know what's at stake."

Ethan shook his head, his frustration evident. "I get that. But this isn't just a story for me—it's my life. My family's legacy. You've put it out there for everyone to dissect, and I'm not sure I'm ready for that."

Claire took a step back, her notebook clutched to her chest. "I didn't mean to hurt you, Ethan. I thought…I thought you trusted me."

"I do," Ethan said, his voice softening slightly. "But trust doesn't make this any easier. You're leaving soon, back to Vancouver, back to your life. You'll move on, but this will still be here—for me, for my family.”

The words stung, but Claire couldn't deny their truth. She looked down, her emotions threatening to overwhelm her. “I never wanted to cause you pain. I just wanted to do justice to the valley, to the people who live here.”

Ethan sighed, running a hand through his hair. “Maybe we just see things differently. You tell stories to connect with people. I try to protect what I care about by keeping it close. Neither way is wrong, but they don't always work together.”

As Ethan turned back to his truck, Claire felt the distance between them widening. She wanted to say something, anything, to bridge the gap, but the words wouldn't come.

“I'll let you get back to work,” she said quietly, her voice barely above a whisper.

Ethan glanced at her, his expression softening slightly, but he didn't stop her as she walked back to her car.

~

Claire drove aimlessly for hours, the familiar roads of the valley blurring as her thoughts churned. Ethan's words replayed in her mind, each one a fresh pang of guilt and frustration. She hadn't meant to betray his trust—she'd only wanted to honor the valley and its stories.

Eventually, she found herself at a quiet overlook, the lake stretching out before her like a vast mirror. She parked and stepped out, the cool air bracing against her flushed cheeks.

Sitting on a boulder, Claire pulled out her notebook and began to write—not for the article, but for herself.

Notebook Excerpt:
This valley is more than its vineyards, more than the people who live here. It's a living, breathing entity, shaped by those who care for it. Ethan's right—it's not just a story. It's a responsibility. And maybe I've overstepped.

But how do you balance truth with respect? How do you tell a story that matters without hurting the people it's about?

As the sun dipped lower, Claire closed her notebook and leaned back, the gentle rustling of the trees soothing her frayed nerves. She thought about the connections she'd built—the people who had trusted her with their stories, the history she'd uncovered.

And then there was Ethan. He wasn't just a source for her article; he had become a part of her story, and she couldn't ignore that.

For the first time, Claire allowed herself to consider the possibility that her time in Kelowna wasn't just a chapter in her career— it was a turning point in her life.

Chapter 52

The following morning, Claire woke to the soft patter of rain against the window, a gray haze shrouding the valley. It matched her mood perfectly. Ethan's words from the previous day still echoed in her mind, a mix of hurt and self-doubt swirling within her.

She sat on the edge of the bed, staring at her laptop. The draft of her article was open on the screen, but for the first time in weeks, the words blurred together, losing the clarity they once had.

A knock at the door pulled her from her thoughts. Margaret stood in the hallway, a knowing look in her eyes.

"You look like you've been wrestling with something," Margaret said, handing Claire a steaming cup of tea.

Claire sighed, taking the cup gratefully. "Ethan and I had a fight. He feels like I crossed a line with my article, and now I don't know if I did the right thing."

Margaret nodded, pulling up a chair. "Sounds like you're both speaking from the heart, but maybe you're not hearing each other clearly."

Later that afternoon, as the rain lightened to a soft drizzle, Claire found herself driving back to Ethan's vineyard. She wasn't sure what she'd say, but she couldn't let things end the way they had.

When she arrived, Ethan was near the barn, sorting through equipment. He looked up, surprise flickering across his face, followed by hesitation.

"Claire," he said simply.

"I need to talk," she said, stepping closer. "If you'll let me."

Ethan set down the wrench he was holding, leaning against the workbench. "I'm listening."

Claire took a deep breath, the weight of her words pressing heavily on her chest. "I've been thinking about what you said. About the article and your family's story. And you're right—it is personal, and maybe I should have handled it differently. But I want you to know that everything I wrote came from a place of respect, of wanting to honor what this valley means to people like you."

Ethan crossed his arms, his expression guarded. "I know that, Claire. But it's hard to see something so personal put out there for the world to judge. This land—it's everything to me. And trusting someone with that isn't easy."

"I understand," Claire said softly. "And I don't want to publish anything that makes you feel like I've betrayed that trust. I can make changes—remove anything you're not comfortable with."

Ethan studied her for a long moment before nodding. "I appreciate that. But it's not just about what's in the article. It's about what happens after. Developers, tourists, critics— they're going to see this valley differently because of what you write. That's what scares me."

Claire stepped closer, her voice steady but earnest. "Ethan, if this article can make people see the valley for what it truly is—a place of history, community, and resilience—then maybe it can help protect it. Maybe it can make them understand why it's worth fighting for."

Ethan's expression softened, a flicker of understanding in his eyes. "You really believe that, don't you?"

"I do," Claire said. "But I also know I can't tell this story without your support. This place is a part of you, and I want to do it justice."

The tension between them eased as Ethan exhaled deeply. "Alright. Let's look at it together. If we're going to tell this story, let's make sure it's the right one."

Claire smiled, relief washing over her. "Thank you."

As they walked toward the house, Ethan glanced at her, a faint smile tugging at his lips. "You're stubborn, you know that?"

Claire laughed softly. "Takes one to know one."

Chapter 53

The hum of the café was a comforting background as Claire sat at her table, laptop open and her fingers hovering over the trackpad. The draft of her article was finally complete, reviewed and approved by Marcy after several back-and-forth revisions. It was scheduled to go live in minutes, and Claire's heart pounded with anticipation and dread.

Ethan had read the final version and given his reluctant blessing. But Claire knew that wasn't the same as wholehearted support. She glanced at her phone, hoping for a message from him, but the screen remained dark.

The digital clock on her laptop clicked over to 10:00 a.m. She refreshed the page of her publication's website, and there it was—her article, front and center, accompanied by a photo of a vineyard bathed in the golden light of sunrise.

The headline read:
"Beneath the Vineyards: The Fight to Preserve the Heart of the Okanagan"
Claire clicked on the link, her own words staring back at her.

Excerpt:
The Okanagan Valley is a landscape of breathtaking contrasts. Rolling vineyards and orchards stretch across sunlit hills, while Okanagan Lake reflects the vibrant hues of every season. It's easy to see why visitors flock here, drawn by the promise of fine wines and serene views. But beneath the surface lies a deeper story—one of resilience, sacrifice, and an enduring connection to the land.

This valley wasn't always covered in grapevines. Long before the first winery was established, the Syilx people lived in harmony with the rhythms of this place. Their traditions, rooted in respect for the land, continue to influence the valley's culture. Generations of settlers followed, drawn by the fertile soil and warm climate, first planting tobacco, then orchards of peaches, apples, and cherries. Each shift in agriculture reflected the adaptability and vision of the people who call this valley home.

Today, the Okanagan is at a crossroads. Development pressures loom large as corporations eye its land for resorts and subdivisions. The allure of progress threatens to erase the very essence of what makes this valley unique.

Ethan Walker, a third-generation winemaker, knows this struggle intimately. His family's vineyard, nestled on a gentle slope overlooking the lake, is a testament to perseverance. "My grandparents planted these vines when people said it couldn't be done," Ethan shares. "They poured their lives into this land, and we've been fighting to keep it ever since."

Ethan's story is not unique. Across the valley, farmers and winemakers grapple with balancing tradition and innovation. Many have faced heart-wrenching decisions—whether to sell to developers or hold onto land that represents generations of hard work.

But it's not just about the economics of agriculture. The Okanagan's vineyards, orchards, and forests hold the memories of those who have nurtured them. A retired orchardist I spoke with recalled frost-bitten winters that tested his resolve, while a young

Syilx elder shared stories of sacred lands and their spiritual significance.

The valley's beauty, it seems, is not just in its landscapes but in the lives entwined with it.

There's a phrase I kept hearing during my time here: beneath the vineyards. It was used to describe the roots of the vines, reaching deep into the earth, but it carries a broader meaning. Beneath the vineyards lie the stories of this valley—the triumphs, the heartbreaks, and the legacies of those who have shaped it.

Preserving the Okanagan isn't just about protecting land or livelihoods. It's about honoring the past while forging a sustainable future. It's about remembering that progress doesn't have to mean destruction.

As I write this, I'm reminded of a moment beneath an old oak tree on Ethan's vineyard. He told me his grandfather believed the land had a soul—that if you listened closely, you could hear its stories.

The Okanagan Valley is speaking. The question is, are we listening?

Her phone buzzed. A text from Marcy appeared:

Marcy:

You nailed it. This is some of your best work. The

depth, the emotion—it's exactly what we needed. Expect some buzz.

Claire exhaled, the praise settling uneasily in her chest. Marcy's approval was gratifying, but it wasn't Marcy's reaction that mattered most.

As the day progressed, Claire watched the article gain traction online. Comments poured in, a mix of admiration and skepticism.

Reader Comments:

> "Beautifully written. Makes me want to visit the Okanagan."
> "Developers are ruining everything. Thank you for shining a light on this."
> "Sounds like a biased piece. Progress is inevitable."

Claire scrolled through, her stomach tightening at the critical ones. She knew this would happen, but it didn't make it easier to see.

By late afternoon, her phone buzzed again. This time, it was Ethan.

Ethan:

Saw the article. You okay?

Claire hesitated before replying.

Claire:

I think so. Are you?

Ethan's reply came quickly:

Ethan:

Mixed feelings, but I think you told it the way it needed to be told.

Relief flooded her, but it was tinged with uncertainty.

That evening, Claire sat on the veranda of the B&B, watching the sun dip below the horizon. Margaret joined her, carrying two cups of tea.

"I read it," Margaret said, settling into the chair beside her. "You've done something important, Claire. People will see the valley differently because of this."

Claire nodded, staring out at the darkening sky. "I hope it's enough to make a difference—and not just bring more pressure."

Margaret placed a comforting hand on her arm. "You've given people a voice. That's all you can do. The rest is up to them."

As the stars appeared, Claire felt a quiet pride mixed with lingering doubt. The article was out there now, its impact rippling through the valley. She didn't know what the future held for Ethan, for the vineyards, or for herself.

But she knew one thing for certain—beneath the vineyards lay a story worth telling, and she had done her best to honor it.

Chapter 54

The golden hues of late afternoon blanketed the valley as Claire arrived at the vineyard hosting the annual harvest festival. The event was Ethan's idea—a way for the community to come together, celebrate the season, and remind everyone of what they were fighting to preserve.

Tables adorned with autumnal decorations stretched across the lawn, laden with fresh bread, cheese, and wine from local producers. Strings of fairy lights crisscrossed overhead, glowing warmly as the sun began its descent. The hum of conversation mingled with the cheerful notes of a live folk band playing under a canopy near the vineyard's edge.

Claire stepped out of her car and took in the scene, her chest tightening with emotion.

This was more than a festival—it was a testament to the valley's resilience and unity.

Ethan spotted her from across the lawn and made his way over, his expression a mix of surprise and warmth.

"You made it," he said, handing her a glass of wine.

"I wouldn't miss it," Claire replied, smiling as she accepted the glass.

They stood together for a moment, watching the crowd. Families mingled with winemakers, and locals greeted each other like old friends. Even the children seemed to understand the importance of the event, their laughter punctuating the air as they darted between rows of vines.

Margaret appeared, carrying a tray of small pastries. "Claire! I'm glad you invited me. Isn't it wonderful?"

"It really is," Claire said, her voice sincere. "I've never seen anything quite like it."

Margaret beamed. "This valley has a way of bringing people together. It's always been that way—through hard times and good."

Ethan nodded. "That's why it's worth fighting for."

As the evening progressed, Claire wandered through the festival, speaking with locals and jotting down notes in her ever-present journal.

She met a retired orchardist who shared tales of frost-bitten seasons and record harvests, and a young couple who had just started their own small winery, inspired by the valley's rich history.

By the time the band struck up its final song, a gentle ballad that seemed to float on the cool night air, Claire found herself near the edge of the vineyard, watching the glow of the festival from a distance.

Ethan joined her, his hands in his pockets as he stood beside her.

"You've been quiet," he said softly.

"Just taking it all in," Claire replied. "This place…these people…it's incredible. I can see why you love it so much."

Ethan smiled, his gaze fixed on the festival. "It's not perfect, but it's home. And nights like this remind me why I fight so hard to keep it that way."

Claire turned to him, her voice filled with conviction. "You're not alone in that fight, Ethan. Your story, the valley's story—it's out there now. People will see what's worth preserving."

He looked at her, his expression unreadable for a moment before softening. "And what about you? Where do you fit into all of this?"

Claire hesitated, the weight of his question hanging between them. "I don't know yet," she admitted. "But I think I'm starting to figure it out."

The music ended, replaced by the murmur of the crowd as the festival began to wind down. Claire and Ethan walked back toward the main area together, their steps unhurried.

For the first time since she arrived in the valley, Claire felt like she belonged—not just as an observer, but as part of the community.

Chapter 55

The soft hum of her phone vibrating on the bedside table jolted Claire awake. She reached for it groggily, blinking at the time—6:45 a.m. The message on the screen was from Marcy.

Marcy:
Fantastic article, Claire. Already generating buzz. Can't wait to discuss your next piece when you're back in the office. Monday, right?

Claire stared at the message, her heart sinking. Monday. Her return to Vancouver was only three days away.

The morning sun crept through the lace curtains of her room, casting soft patterns on the walls. She sat up, hugging her knees to her chest. Her article was out in the world now, and it felt like the culmination of everything she had worked for. But instead of triumph, she felt…unsettled.

The valley had done something to her. Its rhythms, its people, its stories—they'd worked their way under her skin. And then there was Ethan.

By mid-morning, she was on the veranda, sipping tea with Margaret. The older woman studied Claire with her usual perceptiveness.

"You've been quiet," Margaret said.

Claire set her cup down, the weight of her thoughts pressing on her chest. "I'm supposed to go back to Vancouver in a few days. Marcy's already planning my next project."

Margaret nodded knowingly. "But part of you doesn't want to leave."

Claire exhaled deeply, leaning back in her chair. "I didn't expect to feel this way. Kelowna was just supposed to be an assignment—a stepping stone. But now, it feels like more than that."

Margaret smiled gently. "This valley has a way of getting under your skin. It's not just the beauty of the place—it's the people, the stories, the sense of community. Once you've felt it, it's hard to walk away."

Later that day, Claire found herself at Ethan's vineyard, helping him with some end-of-season tasks. The air between them had softened since their earlier conflict, though an unspoken tension lingered.

As they worked side by side, Ethan finally broke the silence. "You're leaving soon."

It wasn't a question, but Claire heard the uncertainty in his voice.

"I don't know," she admitted, brushing her hands on her jeans. "I thought I was. But now…" She trailed off, unsure of how to put her feelings into words.

Ethan stopped what he was doing and turned to face her. "This place changes people, Claire. It shows you things you didn't know you needed. But you have to figure out what it means for you."

She looked at him, her heart pounding. "And what does it mean for us?"

Ethan's gaze softened, but he didn't look away. "That's up to you. I can't tell you to stay—that wouldn't be fair. But I also can't pretend I don't want you to."

That evening, Claire sat by the lake, her journal open on her lap. The Okanagan stretched before her, the water calm and reflective.

Her pen hovered over the page before she began to write:

Journal Entry:
What does it mean to stay? To leave? Vancouver is my home, my career, my familiar. But Kelowna feels like something

new—a place where stories aren't just told but lived.

Ethan says I have to figure out what this place means to me. Maybe the real question is, what do I mean to it?

The thought lingered as she packed up her things and headed back to the B&B. The valley had given her so much—stories, connections, even love. But what could she give back?

As she drifted off to sleep, her decision remained elusive, but the weight of it pressed against her. The clock was ticking, and soon, she would have to choose.

Chapter 56

The early morning sun filtered through the trees, casting dappled light across the veranda where Claire sat. The faint hum of Kelowna waking up drifted in the background—birds chirping, a distant lawnmower, the occasional car passing by. Her laptop rested on the table, open to a blank document.

Her article was already live, making waves she hadn't anticipated. Readers across the country had emailed their reactions, from heartfelt praise to pointed criticism. Yet, as Claire stared at the empty page before her, she felt an urge to write something else—something for herself.

The words came slowly at first but soon began to flow as Claire reflected on the stories she had uncovered.

Journal Entry:

The Okanagan Valley is more than a collection of vineyards and orchards; it is a repository of memories. Each row of vines tells a story, each ripple on the lake a whispered secret. Beneath the vineyards lies the truth of this place—not just its beauty but its soul.

The Syilx people have always known this, their connection to the land a profound testament to harmony and respect. The settlers who came after them carved out lives in the face of unimaginable challenges, planting roots that would feed generations. Today's winemakers carry that legacy forward, balancing tradition with the demands of a modern world.

And yet, beneath the vineyards lies something even deeper—hope. Hope that what has been built will endure, that the sacrifices made by so many will not be in vain.

Claire paused, her fingers hovering over the keys. She thought of Ethan's vineyard, of the stories shared on the bench beneath the oak tree, and the feeling of belonging that had grown stronger with every passing day.

Margaret stepped onto the veranda, a steaming mug in her hand. She placed it beside Claire, her eyes warm with understanding.

"You've found something here, haven't you?" Margaret asked, sitting down across from her.

Claire nodded, her voice soft. "I didn't expect it. I came here for a story, but it's become so much more than that."

Margaret smiled knowingly. "This valley has a way of finding the people who need it most."

As the day stretched on, Claire drove up to Ethan's vineyard one last time. The rows of vines seemed endless, their roots buried deep in the rich soil. She crouched down, running her fingers over the earth, feeling the weight of everything it carried—the past, the present, and the promise of the future.

Ethan found her there, his shadow falling over her as she stood.

"Lost in thought?" he asked, his tone light but his expression searching.

"Something like that," Claire replied. She hesitated before meeting his gaze. "Ethan, I've been thinking about what you said—about the valley, about staying."

He nodded, waiting.

"I don't have answers yet," she admitted. "But I know this place has changed me. It's shown me what it means to belong somewhere, to fight for something that matters."

Ethan's lips curved into a faint smile. "That's enough for now."

They stood together in the quiet of the vineyard, the weight of unspoken words settling comfortably between them. Beneath the vineyards, Claire realized, lay not just roots but connections—between people, between the land and its caretakers, and between herself and a place she never expected to love so much.

Chapter 57

The dawn broke over the Okanagan Valley, a palette of oranges and pinks stretching across the horizon. The stillness of the morning seemed almost reverent, as if the valley itself knew Claire was leaving.

Her bags were packed and loaded into the trunk of her car, but Claire lingered on the veranda of the B&B, a steaming cup of coffee in her hands. The view before her was the same she had admired every day since arriving—rolling vineyards, the glimmering lake, and mountains standing sentinel in the distance. But today, it felt different, sharper, as though every detail had been etched into her memory.

The B&B stood quiet behind her, its charm as comforting as ever. Margaret had hugged her tightly before breakfast, slipping a few lavender scones into her hand "For the road."

Claire smiled and took one, her heart heavy but full. "Thank you. For everything."

Margaret leaned against the railing, her gaze fixed on the valley. "You know, this isn't goodbye. The valley has a way of calling people back. And you, my dear, have left a piece of yourself here."

Claire nodded, the lump in her throat making words impossible. She looked at Margaret, her eyes brimming with gratitude.

Now, with the sun just beginning to crest over the hills, it was time to leave.

Ethan's truck pulled into the driveway as Claire closed the trunk. He stepped out, his hands tucked into his jacket pockets, his expression unreadable.

"You weren't going to leave without saying goodbye, were you?" he asked, his voice tinged with mock reproach.

Claire smiled softly. "I wouldn't do that to you."

They stood in silence for a moment, the weight of unspoken words settling between them.

Ethan shook his head, a faint smile tugging at the corner of his mouth. "I'm not great at goodbyes."

Claire took a step closer, her heart pounding. "Neither am I."

They stood in silence.

"Your article…" Ethan began, his voice quiet but steady. "It's already making waves. People are talking about it, Claire. You've done something important."

Claire felt a swell of pride and sadness. "I didn't do it alone. The valley, its people—you—they gave me the story."

Ethan's gaze met hers, his eyes searching. "You're not just a visitor, Claire. You're part of this now. And maybe, one day…"

He didn't finish the thought, but Claire understood.

She reached out, her fingers brushing against his. "I don't know what the future holds, Ethan. But I know this place will always be a part of me."

Ethan nodded, his hand closing over hers. "And you'll always have a place here. No matter what."

The moment stretched between them, heavy with meaning. Then, without another word, Claire leaned in and kissed him. It wasn't a goodbye—it was a promise, a connection that neither time nor distance could break.

As she drove away, the B&B shrinking in her rearview mirror, Claire felt the tears slip down her cheeks. But they weren't tears of sadness. They were tears of gratitude, of hope, of love.

The valley disappeared behind a bend in the road as she turned on to the Connector, but its essence lingered—its beauty, its people, its stories. Beneath the vineyards, Claire had found something she didn't know she was searching for: a sense of belonging, a connection to something greater.

~

Back in Vancouver, Claire sat at her desk, her laptop open to a new document. The cursor blinked at her, waiting.

She glanced at the photo on her windowsill—Ethan standing in his vineyard, the mountains rising behind him.

The title came to her in an instant, clear and undeniable: Under the Okanagan Sun.

As her fingers began to type, the familiar hum of the city faded. Her mind was back in the valley, in the golden light of its vineyards and the quiet strength of its people.

And somewhere, deep in her heart, she knew her story with Kelowna—and with Ethan—was far from over.

Poems

A Place Called Home

There's a place I long to go
Where the cold winds never blow
It's the place I will always call home,
To the valley of my dreams
And the rippling mountain streams,
Under blue Okanagan skies.

Apple blossoms on the trees
Fill my heart with memories
In the place I will forever call home,
On the shores of golden sand,
Dreamy Ogopogo land,
Under blue Okanagan skies.

When I've wandered far and near,
Used up all my allotted years
Take me back to the place I call home.
Dig my grave upon a hill
Where the sun can warm me still,
Under blue Okanagan skies.

Frank Brummet *(my father-in-law)*

Beautiful Lake Kalamalka

Could there be such a lake as lovely as you?
With your beautiful changing colors of
aquamarine and turquoise.
What is your secret? Some say reflection from
the sky.
Others say minerals below your deep waters.
There are times when you look angry, and
your colors change to darkest green; mostly,
you are serene.

As a child, I admired you, having learned how
to swim in your cool waters.
In my teens, I loved sitting out in a rowboat
listening to the dance music, with a lovely
harvest moon shining above.
At night in our summer cottage, the lapping of
your waves lulled us to sleep.
Sailing along to Cousins Bay for a family
picnic was so much fun.

Even in wintertime, when you were frozen
over,
We learned how to skate by pushing a chair.
They were happy memories that I will always
remember.

Jessie B. Fletcher *(my paternal grandmother)*

Acknowledgments

Writing *Beneath the Vineyards* has been a journey of creativity, self-reflection, and gratitude. This novel would not have come to life without the encouragement, inspiration, and support of many.

First and foremost, I would like to thank my family for their unwavering patience, love, and belief in me. Your support allowed me to immerse myself in the beautiful landscapes of Kelowna and explore the themes of love, healing, and personal growth that shape this story.

A heartfelt thanks to the vibrant Okanagan Valley itself, whose breathtaking vineyards, serene lake views, and welcoming communities served as both the setting and the soul of this novel. The region's charm inspired every scene, and I am deeply grateful for the sense of connection it provided.

To my mentors, colleagues, and fellow writers, thank you for your insights, encouragement, and thoughtful feedback. Your guidance helped me bring this story to life with authenticity and depth.

To my readers, thank you for stepping into the world of *Beneath the Vineyards*. It is my hope that this story not only entertains but also resonates with your own journey of love and transformation.

Finally, I extend my gratitude to the creative spirit that inspired this tale and to the Okanagan heritage that continues to influence my storytelling. Writing *Beneath the Vineyards* has been a celebration of connection, renewal, and the beauty of second chances.

With heartfelt thanks,
Dr. Constance Santego

The Author

Dr. Constance Santego

Dr. Constance Santego is a celebrated author, educator, and holistic healer whose work seamlessly blends storytelling with themes of love, healing, and personal growth. With a doctorate in Natural Medicine and decades of experience in the healing arts, Constance brings a unique depth to her writing, offering readers a journey of both heart and soul.

Born into a family with deep roots in British Columbia—her father's grandparents settling in Vernon in 1912 and her mother's family arriving in Kelowna in 1944—Constance has always drawn inspiration from the rich history and natural beauty of the Okanagan Valley. Her personal connection to the land shines through in her novels, which vividly capture the spirit of the region.

As a writer, Constance combines her academic expertise and love of narrative fiction to craft stories that resonate with readers on a profound level. Her latest work, *Beneath the Vineyards*, invites readers into the sun-soaked vineyards of Kelowna, where themes of resilience, love, and personal transformation unfold against a backdrop of stunning natural beauty and community traditions.

When she's not writing, Constance enjoys life in a serene lakeside community, surrounded by the breathtaking landscapes of Kelowna, British Columbia. Whether exploring local history, guiding others toward personal growth, or simply savoring the quiet moments that inspire creativity, Constance remains dedicated to her mission: to tell stories that heal, uplift, and connect us all.